MADE FOR YOU

Love & Family #2

ANYTA SUNDAY

First published in 2019 by Anyta Sunday,
Contact at Bürogemeinschaft ATP24, Am Treptower Park 24, 12435 Berlin,
Germany

An Anyta Sunday publication
http://www.anytasunday.com

ISBN 978-3-947909-11-7

Cover Design: Natasha Snow

Line Editor: HJS Editing

This book contains sexual content.

To my wonderful son.
You challenge and elate me, and I learn from you every single day.

Chapter One

BEN

I GROGGILY HOP INTO MY CLOSET-SIZED KITCHEN, STRUGGLING into a pair of tight jeans. "Milo! We're late, fuck."

"*You're* late, you mean."

My eleven-year-old brother is squeezed behind a two-person dining table. Cocoa Puffs carpet the surface and milk has spilled over his gold-and-navy school uniform.

I snap my top button and reach for a bowl. I tip the box, and a few measly puffs fall out.

Pray to God there's Fanta in the fridge.

I lurch across the kitchen, and Milo snickers. "There's no Fanta in the fridge."

The day just turned disastrous.

"How many cans did you drink?"

Milo jerks a hand toward the empty cereal box. "There was only half a bowl."

I search the messy table and count two cans of Fanta,

tipped sideways. "If you'd poured the Cocoa Puffs into your bowl and not around it, you'd have filled it. And I wouldn't have to go to my dead-end day job a cranky ass."

"You think Fanta would have changed that?"

"Smart ass. Grab your bag, it's time for school."

Milo pokes his tongue out. "Favorite part of your day, isn't it?"

"Especially on days you drink my Fanta." I poke my tongue back at him.

"You have a problem, Benny."

"More than one, bucko."

He eyes my bright ginger hair and winces. "Yeah."

I laugh, and choke on a rank smell filling the air. Milo's lips lift into a guilty grin. "Farts wouldn't smell so bad if we moved into the main house. The extra space would thin them out."

It's not Milo's first attempt to evict us from the 200-square-foot guest cottage at the back of our property, but it's the smelliest.

Okay, our bedrooms are tiny. And yes, the bathroom is only a cabinet shower and toilet, so we use the kitchen sink to wash our hands. But we have a dishwasher. Yay for the little things?

Milo flashes me puppy-dog eyes. "Pleeeaase? I want my old room back."

I swallow. "Not a conversation to have while I'm bereft of Fanta."

"Bereft?"

"Lacking. Empty of."

Milo shoots me a finger-gun—just like Dad used to do. "You might be bereft of Fanta, but I am not bereft of fantasy."

I stop plucking Cocoa Puffs from the table and stare at my little brother. It's weird to see myself mirrored in him. It's gotten more and more over the last year. I'm kinda proud, and I'm kinda worried. Like, I don't know what the fuck I'm doing, but at least his wit is improving?

I chuck the cereal bits into my mouth and grab my keys. "Ass up and out the door."

Milo stubbornly sinks into his seat and rivets his eyes on me.

"I mean it, bucko."

He doesn't budge. "Shouldn't you be wearing your Te Papa T-shirt?"

I snort. "Like hell I'm wearing that a minute before I have to."

He studies my shirt, and suddenly I wish I were wearing the ugly turquoise-and-white polo. He reads aloud, "Say Please and I'll Bend Over?"

I wince.

This is what sleepless nights do to me. I didn't even think about what I shoved on.

"It means that I'll bend over backward. You know, be extra helpful to anyone with good manners."

Milo isn't fooled. "You should play harder to get."

Heat rips up my throat. Dammit. How was I meant to respond? How would Mum and Dad have responded?

Of course, they wouldn't have needed to, because they'd never have worn such a suggestive shirt.

I swing my keys over my finger and eye the exit. "Look, someday you'll discover you have . . . feelings, and it's important to know these feelings aren't bad. Expressing them isn't a bad thing—as long as everyone involved wants it, and you're safe. You know?"

Milo eyes my discomfort, making his eyes glint. Whoever said what goes around, comes around was right.

Milo was me, twelve years ago, blatantly egging our parents on while Milo was crying in the cradle.

"I don't know," Milo says, still unskilled at schooling his smirk. "Why don't you tell me more?"

"Not on an empty stomach." I grab my wallet from its spot next to the toaster. "How much to move your butt to the car?"

"Twenty bucks."

"You sure aren't bereft of fantasy." I toss him two dollars.

He catches it and hauls himself out the door. "It's not fantasy," he says quietly as we pass the main house en route to the car, gravel crunching underfoot. "I want my old room back."

I tuck him against my side, my sigh skipping through his floppy, blond hair. "I thought I paid you to stop with the uncomfortable conversations."

He peers up at me. "Some are priceless."

"I need a drink."

We stop at a store on the drive to Kresley Intermediate School. Milo jumps out, telling me to stay put. He returns jiggling a bottle of my favorite orange soda. "Drink up."

I snap the cap and take a delightful sip. It fizzes over my tongue, down my throat, and, within moments, it bubbles through my veins. Fantastic stuff.

My brother has lost his cheeky grin and is staring out the passenger window. It's a glimpse of the tender, grieving kid who—like me—hides behind humor.

I want to reach out and acknowledge this side of Milo, like I wish someone would with me, but I don't know how.

"This drink is almost as sweet as you, bro."

He shrugs. "None of my teachers think I'm sweet."

"Pfft. Teachers. What do they know."

"Multiplication, the capital of Australia, how to build a birdhouse."

"I can count, the capital of Australia is Canberra, you got me on the birdhouse."

Milo snorts. "The capital of Australia is Sydney. Everyone knows that."

I wince. My brother is so confident. And so wrong. Parent-teacher night will be a fun evening. "My point is: none of them know you like I do."

Milo folds his arms dramatically. "My life just got so sad."

I pull out into traffic and stall. A bus honks behind me.

I curse and restart, aware of Milo tensing. Driving isn't our favorite pastime.

I flash him a soothing smile to let him know I have it under control, and promise myself to get the car checked this weekend.

The bus honks again when I slow for an orange light.

"That driver has a hard-on for you, huh?"

"Watch your language." The bus honks another time. "Has a hard-on, all right."

When we park outside Kresley Intermediate, Milo stares reluctantly at the swarms of kids.

I don't want to rush him, but the dashboard clock reminds me I have to be dressed and sporting a charmed smile in twenty minutes. Traffic through the tunnel is a nightmare at this hour.

I help myself to more Fanta. "What's up, Milo?"

"I saw your laptop last night. It was open, and I looked when you were in the bathroom."

I freeze.

Kill. Me. Now. "This is awkward."

"Why didn't you tell me?"

It's not like I've denied being gay, it just . . . never came up. I shrug. "Didn't think it was important."

"It is. I hate it."

I grip the bottle, the plastic slipping against my suddenly sweaty hand. "You don't get a say in it, Milo. I will live my life the way I need to."

"It's selfish. Mum and Dad would hate it."

There's not enough Fanta in the world to ease that hit.

My throat and voice tighten. "Well. Now they'll never know."

Milo's bottom lip wobbles, and I'm torn between my own hurt and wanting to soothe his.

I'm totally screwing up the most important job Mum and Dad left me with. "Let's chat about this later, yeah?"

Milo climbs out, bends back inside, and steals my Fanta. "Buy more. We're gonna need it."

Chapter Two

JACK

As this kid's teacher, I'm not supposed to laugh.

But it's hard not snorting at the ludicrous things Milo says to his mate Devansh during my forty-minute woodwork class.

"Get your own nails, birch."

I spare Milo a look over the table cluttered with uneven birdhouses.

"What?" Milo flashes me all his teeth. "Birch is a wood. It's totally classroom appropriate—"

"Quit it," I say, continuing to sand a detached doorknob.

There are heaps of reasons I have Milo working at my table. Pretty much all of them have to do with the uncensored shit that comes out of him.

Definition of potty mouth? Eleven-year-old Milo McCormick.

After a few parental complaints, the school principal urged

all his teachers to keep a short leash on him. We're doing our best, but it's hard to be too strict on the kid.

It's only been a year since his parents' car plummeted over Rimutaka Hill Road, killing them. Everyone knows it. The damn whole of New Zealand knows of the McCormick crash. Headlines blasted over every news channel the day it happened, a poignant reminder to drive safely over the Easter holidays.

This is my first year with Milo, but from what his primary school teachers passed on to Kresley Intermediate, he'd been a quiet kid. Before.

I can barely believe it.

"It's my religious belief that all extra-terrestrials have wangs the length of this ruler."

Christ. Not laughing will kill me.

I cut him another look. "That's a level, not a ruler. Less talking and more hammering."

Milo snickers to his buddy with a gesture I'm glad not to catch. "I could hammer this all night long."

Where was the bell when you needed it?

"Longer, if I were extra-terrestrial. Or Jesus."

A snort escapes me, and I cover it with a cough. I'm certain this kid knows nothing of religion.

"Ten minutes until the end of class," I tell him. "Don't talk until then."

"Or what?"

My rough-sounding empty threats mean nothing to this kid.

"Or I'll make you and Devansh clean the woodwork station before I let you go."

"You always make us clean the woodwork station before we go."

I try to hide my fond exasperation. My reputation as a no-

bullshit teacher counts on it. "*All* of the woodwork stations—"
I sense a scoff and add—"And all the sawdust collecting in
the bins."

This seems to work, and I file the threat away for
future use.

When the bell rings, all the kids file out except Milo. He
fiddles with the level, slumped on his stool.

I pack away forgotten nails and hammers from the five
classroom stations. Milo keeps glancing at me. I sidle to his side
of the working station. "What's up, Milo?"

"Tonight is parent-teacher night." He flinches.

I grip the sawdust-filmed bench and crouch to eye level.
"So it is."

He averts his gaze. "My brother Ben's coming."

Mrs. Devon had already told me she'd demanded Ben
McCormick visit. Apparently, Mrs. Devon had been Ben's
teacher a dozen years ago and now recognized Milo's behavior
as identical to his brother's. *Someone* had to tell Ben he was a
bad influence and an unfit legal guardian.

"I was thinking," Milo says, "maybe you could chat
with him?"

"Want me to show him your work?"

He shrugs. "Nah, I mean, whatever."

Most parents don't bother meeting with extra-curricular
teachers on parent-teacher night, but we all hang out in the
classroom in case a parent pops in. I'm thrilled at the idea of
Milo's brother talking with me, because woodwork is the only
class Milo's actively taking a part in. I can give his brother
something positive to take home.

Because honestly? Behind all the birches and religious
beliefs? Milo is a grieving boy who craves attention.

"What do you want me to chat with your brother about?"

Milo blinks furiously, jaw tight like he's fighting tears. Like he's trying hard to play the role of a tough, smart-mouthed kid. Sympathy wrenches through me. He's a kid.

He's just a kid.

"I'm here for you, Milo. I'm listening. What's going on?"

Milo's voice breaks as he blurts out his request.

Chapter Three

BEN

WHERE THE HELL IS WING C?

I stall in the quiet quad, stomach knotting, unknotting, and knotting again. I'm already five minutes late, and even though I recognize half the buildings from when I attended Kresley Intermediate, I have no clue where to go. Wing C? I didn't even know there was a Wing C.

Jesus, it's quiet. Did I calendar the wrong date? Or did all the other parents arrive on time like responsible adults?

I breathe in a salty breeze and wish I were a seagull circling overhead so I could find the building I'm meant to be in.

Mrs. Devon would probably still kick my ass. Unless she's softened with age?

Maybe she'd cut me some slack if I explained that my car stalled up the hill and I had to coast in neutral—and terror— all the way down here.

I can only hope.

My best bet? The long brightly painted building? Or the taller one?

More lights were on in the taller building.

A path winds around a semi-cordoned off grassy-stretch, but I dash over the boggy grass. I'll save every minute I can—

My foot skids on a slick patch, and I'm whipped onto my ass with a wet, heavy slap. I brace against the cold ground, weeds and sludge slurping between my fingers.

With a shaky laugh, I push to my feet.

Some days sure test my fortitude.

"Shortcuts never end well."

I whirl around. A dozen yards away, a male figure is casually leaning over a ramp leading to the craft rooms. The setting sun behind the building makes it difficult to see details.

I wipe the globs of mud from my good jeans. "You don't say."

He laughs. "Hang on. I'll get you a towel."

The man—either a teacher or a very at-home parent— ducks inside the small building.

It's not at all in the direction of the building I was aiming for, but I can't trek all this mud into a kid's classroom, and maybe this guy can give me directions.

I make it to the ramp just as my towel-wielding savior emerges. Bright eyes track over me with barely suppressed laughter.

He tosses me the towel. "Go nuts."

I scrub myself down quickly. A chunk of mud juts out from my boot heel and there's no way around it but to smear it onto the towel. I'm getting an eyeful of this guy's feet, and I have to say, he has perfected the lumber-man style. Metal-capped boots, jeans, and a flannel shirt.

I straighten. He's fit, and he exudes manliness: broad shoulders, blunt jaw with a hint of six o'clock shading, and thick brows.

Compelling green eyes twinkle good-naturedly, softening the innate strength in his face. He lifts a brow, and I grin. "What's the protocol here? Do I give this back to you, or take it home to wash first?"

He gestures for the towel—more brown now, than blue—and his large hand closes around it. "Where are you heading?"

"Wing C. There's a mad hen waiting to rip out my throat and feast on my entrails."

"Mrs. Devon?"

I cock him a finger-gun. I am my dad's son. "Five points to Gryffindor."

He gestures toward the soccer pitch. "Behind the gym."

I jog down the ramp and into the quad. "Wish me luck."

His chuckle follows me as I make a dash for it. "You'll need more than luck wearing that shirt."

Fuck. The shirt. I knew I forgot something.

Around a darkened corner of the small building, I turn it inside out, mud sticky and cold against my skin. Mrs. Devon gives off her usual Professor Snape vibe when I enter the classroom. I sling myself into the chair that sits opposite her paper-crammed desk.

Looking at her is like diving back in time. She is wearing the same style woolen cardigan and large glasses that make her accidentally fashionable. She clicks the strap of her silver watch against the desk.

"Jesus, you haven't changed a bit, Mrs. Devon."

Her eyes narrow. "Benjamin Jeremiah McCormick. It seems you haven't changed either."

My stomach buzzes with sudden nausea. Is she about to tell me I'm doing a bad job raising Milo?

Tell me anything else.

I can't hear that.

I'm afraid I'm doing a bad job, too.

Chapter Four

JACK

I'M SITTING AT MY WORKSTATION, BOWED OVER A SCHOOL laptop, searching the internet for real estate. I need to move out from my last remodeling project. Stat. I sold the house to my ex, Luke and his partner Sam, and we've been co-living the last week. While our dynamic is great, I'm not fond of sharing a wall with the lovebirds. It's painfully awkward.

Time to find a small, rundown house to renovate. Something manageable and temporary.

Something to kill time until I buy my dream home. The one that I've been saving for the last eight years.

The one I'll buy when the owner finally sells.

Nothing else punches me with inspiration.

Someone clears their throat.

I jump, whacking my elbow on the table. Nice funny-bone hit. I swallow a hiss and glance over. My jiggling pulse settles.

Not Milo's brother.

I exchange a few words with the curious Dad before he leaves. A few more parents come in, but still no Ben McCormick.

I glance at the clock. Seven. Interviews should have wrapped up by now.

I wait an extra ten minutes, in case he is running late.

The tickly feeling in my gut says Ben was the young, red-haired guy I met earlier. The one in the unfortunate T-shirt, covered in mud, wincing at the mention of Mrs. Devon. I wish I'd asked. Wish I'd used the moment to chat with him about Milo's passionate outburst.

I clean up my station and lock up. A salty breeze ushers me to the back of the school where I park my truck—it takes up a lot of space and there isn't enough staff parking as it is.

It's almost dark, a purplish tinge to the sky, and street lamps gaze between picket fences.

Usually there's no sound save a whistling breeze and the clap of my boots. Not tonight.

Across the road, under the shadows of a pohutakawa tree, a familiar figure lifts the bonnet of his hatchback. He's all lean angles and mud-caked jeans, and the soles of his calf-hugging boots are French-kissing a puddle.

His voice carries. "Okay, what am I looking at?"

He fishes out his cell phone, and bright light hits his face. "Google. Why the fuck doesn't my car start?"

I grin. Generation Z.

He laughs at whatever flashes on screen. The sound is both bright and exhausted.

"Great lot of help you are." He stuffs his phone into his back pocket and bends toward the engine. Like sniffing the grease will magically convert him into a mechanic.

I cross the road to him. "How's it going there?"

He jerks his head up and I catch the bonnet and lift it before he whacks his head. He blinks. Then cranks out a hollow laugh. "Well, I'm not bleeding on the outside. Yet."

Wariness lurks in his dark eyes. Such a difference from the harried frustration he'd carried earlier. What the hell did Mrs. Devon tell him? "Calling it a good day, huh?"

He snorts. "The best. But it's only quarter past seven. It still has time to make the top three."

His sarcasm is crisp, and I brace against the pained undercurrents. "What's your plan?"

"For making it to the top three? I don't know, but I suspect begging Towel Guy for a lift will be part of it."

"Jack." I don't know why I tell him my first name. Something to ponder later. "If I'm right, I have your brother Milo in my class."

He slicks on a tight smile, and steps back stiffly. This is Ben, all right. "Look, I'm sorry if he's a handful. I know I'm fucking up, okay? Just, please. No more flagellation tonight."

My grip on the bonnet is so hard, it will leave a lasting imprint on my palm. "Hang on, mate. Milo's an amazingly spirited kid with fantastic imagination, and he's quick. He has potential to do great things, and I am happy he's in my class."

Ben softly hiccups, then covers it with a laugh. "Really?"

My chest twists. Milo uses the same defense mechanism.

I study Ben McCormick. He must be a decade older than Milo, and I'd guess at least a dozen years younger than myself. He's tall, almost my height, but carries the leanness of a guy in his twenties. His muddy clothes stick to him, showing off an enviable frame. His hair is possibly the brightest ginger I've seen in my life, but the shock of color is tempered by dark eyes. Eyes that fasten to my jaw, weighted with emotion.

He shivers in the chilling night. The cold bites through my dry clothes. He must be freezing in his damp ones.

"Milo is a good kid." There's more to bring up, but first

things first. "I'm out a set of jumper cables. I'll taxi you home if you like?"

Ben sighs. "Thank fuck I didn't have to beg." He snaps down the bonnet. "You had me on my toes a minute there." He sidles past me, and I inhale a lungful of his clean scent.

I take a quick step back.

He retrieves a six-pack of Fanta from the back seat of his car and I lead him to the truck. "Where to?"

"Wainuiomata."

"*Wainui?*" That was a good hour from here.

A small—very small—spark hits his eyes. "I'm shitting you. I'm in Berhampore, five minutes over the hill."

He jumps into the truck, fingers trembling as he plants the soda between us. I'm not convinced it's all to do with the cold.

"You're Milo's teacher?"

I run my hands over the grainy wheel. "Mr. Pecker. He takes my woodwork elective."

"*You're* Mr. Pecker?" Ben's voice hops on a laugh. He realizes and slams his eyes shut. "Sorry. Some adult I make."

I shift on my chair, stomach twisting with sympathy. So much expectation and responsibility had been cast onto the guy, and so young. I'm angry at Mrs. Devon for criticizing him. Clearly, Ben is trying. Hell, he came to the parent-teacher night —and that's more than some parents manage.

His posture wars between defeat and stubborn desperation to keep it together. If anyone needs some slack, it's this guy.

"It's okay to laugh."

He eyes me dubiously. "Really?"

"My name's *Pecker*. Really."

He cocks a thick brow, darker orange than his hair. "Do the kids tease you mercilessly?"

"I have a staple gun sitting on my desk." I start the engine. "The only kid brave enough to risk it is your brother."

Ben chokes between laughter and mortification. "He *doesn't.*"

"He calls me Mr. Woodpecker."

Ben slumps with relief. Not quite the parentally concerned response I'm used to. "Oh, thank God. I thought he was talking about your dick."

Definitely not the response I'm used to.

I scrub a palm over a smirk. No surprise where Milo's potty mouth comes from. These brothers are birds of the same feather.

We pause at the T-junction leading to the main road.

Ben casts a none-too-regretful look to the school before I turn. "Twenty-four. A degree in environmental economics. And school is still not behind me."

I laugh. This guy is easy to like.

A little too easy.

I remind myself that I'm a teacher, and he is a caregiver of a student in my class. Probably still grieving. And a decade and a half too young.

"I was hoping you'd come in and speak with me tonight."

Ben rubs his nape. "I reached the limit."

"I get it, Mr. McCormick."

"Ben!"

I'm relieved at the correction. "I get it, Ben."

"This is what adults do, though, isn't it? They listen even if it breaks their heart."

He sinks back in the seat and curls his feet against the vinyl. So tenderly at home.

He rubs his shirt, which I noticed with earlier bemusement is inside out. He obliviously rakes his fingers over his hard nipple, and I jerk my gaze to the wet road.

"Before you hit me with whatever Milo's done," he says. "Can you do me a favor?"

"What did you have in mind?"

"Tell me what a composed adult's day looks like?"

He's so lost, yet he takes it in good stride. And that smile is maddeningly charming.

I tighten my grip on the wheel. "There's no one-size fits all example."

"What does your day look like?"

"My circumstances are completely different than yours."

He huffs, like he thinks I'm making excuses for him. I'm not. I call things as I see them. Perhaps with a better filter.

"I'm a single guy with no kids and no home." I clear my throat. "You're caring for an eleven-year-old. Escalating hormones are hard enough to deal with. You're managing a host of additional emotions. Milo's still coming to terms with losing your mum and dad."

Ben stills.

"And I suspect you are, too."

His breath hitches.

"We want to support Milo as best we can."

"We?"

"We teachers. This evening was meant to plan for that. Not to chastise you." I give him an encouraging smile. "You're doing your best."

Ben's eyes shimmer. His expression flickers with relief. He smiles. It's brief, but there, and he surprises me with his strength by facing me. No ducking his chin or shying away. He looks at me with a rush of trust that I've not experienced for a long time.

"Tell me what Milo did."

Chapter Five

BEN

I'm doing my best. I'm doing my best.

It aches, hearing someone recognize it, but it doesn't dull the nagging question: is my best enough?

Jack speaks, voice enviably collected, "Milo approached me after class today—"

"Wait—mentally prepping—Is this worse than the Woodpecker thing?"

"It's nothing he's done. It's something bothering him at home."

I *tsk*. "You were supposed to ease the tension, Jack. Not make me want to throw up."

Jack's lips hitch. "How about this. I tell you the facts, and you respond. No judgements. Preferably roll down the window, first."

I rub my palms along my thighs and screw up the guts to hear him out. "Lay it on me."

"Milo is upset at something he saw on your computer—"

"*What?*" I can't believe it. Milo talking about *that* to a teacher is so beyond okay. I want to be understanding, but this makes me furious. "He snuck into my room when I was in the bathroom. I didn't leave it out where he could just see it. I'm not *totally* irresponsible. I could have sworn I'd clicked it away."

"Ben," Jack say calmly, but there's nothing calm about this.

My mind conjures a pretty picture of my brother—and my hands strangling his silly little neck. "What did he tell you? That I need to change? That he'll run away if I don't? Or will he tell the authorities I suck at looking after him—"

"Ben." Jack's no-bullshit tone halts me. His face appears both horrified and bemused. "That was a lot of information to process, and still not enough to make any sense."

I open my mouth and he slants me a look. I shut it and listen.

"I promised no judgements, but you've got to let me finish."

"You must think I'm the least qualified person to raise a preteen."

Jack hits the windshield wipers. "Zero points to—?"

"A clipped Ravenclaw," I answer. Wait, zero points?

Our eyes connect for a moment, and the air crackles.

Misty rain has filmed the passenger window. The heat has kicked on inside the truck, and despite the failure pooling in my gut, I feel safely cocooned.

Jack's eyes track the road. He stops at stop signs. Slows for orange. Carefully steps on the brake. Never stalls.

It's lulling.

Like it could help me finally sleep.

"Milo saw you looking into real estate agents."

I rake a hand through my hair and laugh. "I'm such a fucking idiot. *That's* what he saw?"

Jack's hands shift on the wheel, veins prominent. "I don't dare ask what you thought he saw."

"I don't dare tell you!"

Jack's laughter is full-hearted, deep, and infectious. "He asked if I could somehow stop you from selling."

"Why would he think you could stop me?"

Those green eyes snuck to mine. "It's known around school that I'm into renovation and remodeling. I just sold my last place to our gym teacher."

"Was that what you meant by having no home?"

Jack tenses, and quickly inclines his head. "Sure."

There's more to it. I'm a questionable influence, not emotionally clueless.

I know better than to pry. Usually. "Where are you living?"

"Newtown. Sharing a wall with my ex and his partner, and on the hunt for a new project." He winks, and I'm not immune to its power. Especially on the heels of that insight.

Milo's teacher. Milo's gay teacher.

Milo's ruggedly hot, gay teacher.

I pre-emptively confess my sins. I'm taking the image of his steady gaze, curved lips, and work-toughened hands to bed tonight.

"Milo believed if I remodeled, the house would be different enough that you'd stay."

What an effective bucket of ice.

Will Milo ever give up?

Can't he accept it's too hard to live there? "That's painfully naïve."

"You've got to give the kid credit for trying."

I lift the Fanta onto my lap. Sure going to need this tonight. "Left. Here on the corner."

Jack eases into a free parking spot directly outside my house, and his gaze jerks past me to our property. His eyes dance, and he wrings his hands on his wheel with a contradictory groan.

I look from him to the house and back again. "What's wrong?"

Chapter Six

JACK

WHAT'S WRONG?

Ben and Milo's house is a beautiful 1920s bungalow.

It's a large corner-street property with low-pitched single roofs, projecting rafters at gable ends, and big bow windows.

It is crying for new paint, the garden is wild and out of control, and vines are creeping up the corner of house.

One look, and I'm fueled with the itch to fix it. Ben is staring at me, puzzled. "You've got to clear the ivy from your exterior walls." I readjust my hands on the wheel. "The roots can compromise the foundations of the house, mess with your drainage systems."

"Add that to the growing to-do list I will never get around to."

I wince, half-tempted to dash across the yard and start pulling ivy. But this is his house. It's none of my business. "If you decide to sell, clear them first. A makeover will increase the return on your investment." Is that stained-glass window trimming? The house has ridiculous potential—

Christ, there's a kid on the roof.

Ben sees Milo's darkened figure balancing the supporting beam too. He yanks off his belt and we hit the path to his house. In the near distance, a woman is screaming at Milo to come down. We hurtle down the side of the house, gravel pinging off our boots and against the fence.

It's instinct to follow. To lend a hand. I'd do it for anyone, but it's Milo on the roof, and my heart is hammering. I need this kid's feet to hit the ground safely.

Ben yells for Milo to get his ass down. A middle-aged lady in an oversized coat glares at him. "Did he pull the ladder up with him again?"

She hikes past us in barely restrained rage. "That's the last time I'm babysitting your brother. Get a grip on him, Ben. Your parents would be sorely disappointed."

Ben balks. The sound of her feet trudging through gravel slowly fades. I want to chase after her and tell her off for having no tact. For being so insensitive.

But there's a kid climbing onto the gable, demanding attention.

Moonlight washes over an untamed garden, an add-on guest cottage, and Milo sulking on the roof, back turned.

I spot a trellis wrapped with long dead tomato vines.

I'm eager to whip out my no-bullshit teacher voice and yell at Milo to listen, quick and smart. But I'm aware that behind Ben's schooled face, he's panicking about being a terrible brother. Taking these reins from him would crush his confidence.

Still. I give the trellis a sturdy shake. Always good to have a plan B.

Ben throws me a weak grin. "Does he still get credit for trying?"

I hook my fingers into the trellis, ready but waiting.

Ben plucks a lemon off a bushy tree. I'm not convinced this is his cleverest idea, but I bite my tongue. He throws the lemon and it smacks against the shingles a few feet from Milo.

Milo whips his head toward the sound and spots the fruit rolling into the gutter. "Are you trying to kill me?" he shouts indignantly.

Ben shouts back, "If life gives you lemons, throw them until your brother gets off the bloody roof."

Another lemon flies over Milo's head. He ducks and dramatically hugs his body against the shingles.

I'm not going to lie. The scene amuses me.

It also tugs at a tender wound.

As a kid—hell, as a twenty-year-old—I always imagined having a big, loud family. I imagined shared dinners and over-shared stories. Imagined fights and ridiculous gestures to make up for them. I imagined living in a house that I'd slaved over and a husband to laugh with during the day and moan with during the night.

Instead, I got my parents and brothers turning their backs.

I shake off the memory, clutching the trellis hard enough to invite splinters.

Ben has given up on the lemons. "Come down or I'll drink all the Fanta." He eyes me, and his whisper carries the six feet between us. "Could you grab them from the truck? Seeing is believing and all that."

I don't particularly want to leave these boys out of my sight, but I dash to the truck.

When I return, Milo is finally facing Ben. "I don't want you to sell the house."

"Look, it won't happen immediately. But it will happen."

"It's not fair."

"Not got the memo yet, bucko? Life isn't fair."

They stare at each other. I don't want to break their moment, but a twig snaps underfoot.

Milo spots me and his body jerks with surprise. "Mr. Woodpecker?"

Ben smirks before turning his chin toward Milo. I think he might tell him to cut that nicknaming shit out.

"Mr. Woodpecker holds your Fanta ransom."

Or not.

I'm close to ending this standoff and barking orders. If Milo were my kid, I'd have his ass in bed and restricted from media for two weeks.

Not my kid. Not my kid.

Ben reads my face and his expression shutters. "Fuck. We're pissing off your teacher. How much will it take to get you down?"

He pulls a wallet from his back pocket.

"Fifty," Milo hollers.

"Five."

"Forty."

This is not actually happening. Ben's parenting is unorthodox at best.

"Ten."

"Thirty-five, and not a dollar less."

"Fifteen, and you shower before bed."

Milo leans over the edge and reins in his shout. "Do I have to do my hair?"

Poor Ben is damp and muddy and miserable, and Milo needs to quit this charade.

I catch Milo's gaze and hold it. It might not be my place, but I have to do something for Ben. My voice is steady and commanding. "Get your butt down here, boy. Or I'll have you cleaning the class bins all week."

"Fine. Fifteen bucks. I'll do my hair." He lowers a rickety

ladder and I brace it as he climbs down.

Ben crowds close behind me, warming my back. He lets out a breathy 'thank fuck' at my nape that feels a lot like brushing against an electric line that definitely shouldn't be crossed.

Chapter Seven

BEN

I LEAVE WORK AT THE NATIONAL MUSEUM WITH A HEADACHE AND blink in the bright autumn day as I tromp toward my car. The harbor dazzles with sunlight and makes my head pound.

Gulls overhead squawk something vicious.

The painkiller better kick in quickly.

It's been a week since parent-teacher conferences and my world is spiraling out of control. Funny, because everything I'm doing is supposed to mitigate that.

Instead, my manager Gemma threw a fit when I requested a thirty-hour week schedule to spend more quality time with Milo. No more of him bussing to and from school. I gotta pick him up. Use the time to chat through school issues, look at his homework, take him out for me-him afternoons.

The response I got was: *Other people manage life with a full-time workload.*

It's a horrible thought, but I hope she has kids and regrets those words.

Clearly I'm pissed because she has a point. Other people *do* manage kids with a full-time workload.

It feels shitty to admit I can't. To beg for the time.

That run-in would be enough to give me a headache, but the house dilemma is also weighing on me.

Milo begging to move back to his old room.

Milo refusing to talk to me since I had an agent look at the property two days ago.

He still won't talk to me, even though it's not likely we'll sell anytime soon. The agent was lovely but direct: renovating the place first would be ideal. At the very least, a good spruce up.

I settle inside my car and repeat my mantra. "You've got this. You've got this."

I power pose, arms lifted above my head. I drum-punch the bumpy car ceiling.

It helps, but what I need is the fizzling, fantastication that is Fanta.

A good fuck would also do wonders but scoring that seems laughably implausible. Like, who with?

More to the point, when?

Staring at a ferry docking in the blinding harbor, I call my best friend Talia.

It's a ridiculous hour in Europe, and she'll have her phone off. So I leave a message.

"Talia, babe. It's your best mate, remember me?" I exaggerate a sigh. "Europe is too much competition, I get it. Tell me what you're up to. What cute guys are in your life. Let me live vicariously through you, because I'm hard up here.

"Sending you kisses. Send some back please. From you. From any hot guys . . . I don't mind."

I want to say 'dick pics welcome' but I'm a year and one fatal car crash more mature than that.

I hang up and start the car. It revs to life smoothly with its new battery, and I'm relieved.

At the Newtown Mall, I'm tempted to grab a Fanta and fuck off, but the food supply is low at home and I should probably do the whole shopping thing. Using my weekly free hour for myself is a pipedream. But as the French so charmingly put it: *C'est la vie.*

If I race through the supermarket, maybe I'll have twenty minutes for a shower and a quick wank before playing adult again.

"Out of the way!" I call to a group of uniformed high school kids discussing who looked old enough to buy wine. I race past, then pause at the request of my moral compass. "Might consider ditching the uniforms, guys."

Male laughter drifts across the aisle. Good luck to the teens if half the supermarket can hear them plot. I refuse to believe I was ever so stupid, but I'm sure Talia would remind me otherwise.

Milk, cereal, and Fanta land in the cart. Followed by a dozen microwave meals. I zip toward the fresh meat counter. If I stock the fridge with sausage meat, I could use it to bribe Milo to speak to me again. He loves chicken with peas.

Like always, there's a line. I weigh the cost/benefit of enticing Milo to speak to me versus enjoying a nice, hot shower.

I sigh.

No matter the temptation, I will always choose my bucko.

The universe rewards me.

Trundling around the corner toward the meat counter is Milo's hot woodwork teacher.

Jack's gait is steady and solid. His well-trimmed dark hair gleams under harsh supermarket lighting. I pegged him as older our first meeting, but other than gentle weathering around those bright eyes and tough skin at his hands, he looks younger. Mid-thirties maybe.

His eyes clasp on me, and he startles into a slow smile. He fans his fingers in an acknowledging wave. "Ben McCormick," he says as he lines up behind me.

"Jack Pecker," I reply. "You cutting school?"

His laughter leaps into the air, and I recognize it as the heavy, seductive laugh I heard around the wine-plotting teens. "Thirty-hour work week at Kresley. Today's a half day." Jack's phone buzzes. "Excuse me a sec."

He checks his message, and types back. I take advantage of the moment and admire his prominent profile. His nose is sharp, and his wide mouth is set with a stubborn edge matching his hard chin. Definitely the jaw of a teacher who takes cheek from no one. Yet his eyes blaze with good humor and calm.

My gaze scrolls over his unbuttoned flannel shirt, rolled up at the sleeves. The green and black checkered fabric looks worn and soft and probably smells of his woodsy scent. Underneath he's wearing a Swandri T-shirt that clings to his tapered frame.

The cart disrupts the view, but I glimpse dark canvas work-pants flecked with oil stains, and heavy boots.

A dark brow juts upward and his gaze drills questioningly into me.

It galvanizes me into speech. "I'm in the market for"—I whisk a finger toward his chest—"new T-shirts. Impressionable minds at home and all."

His lips hop at the edges. "How's it going with Milo?"

"Costing me a fortune to keep him in line."

"Have you considered other methods? Limiting TV time, giving him extra chores?"

"This is the twenty-first century. If he wants media, he can find it." I glance sideways, lower my voice, and share my hard-earned wisdom. "Kids have all the power."

Jack's laugh is cut off when his phone rings.

He lifts a finger in the universal sign of 'one moment' and answers. Apparently he's making dinner for four, and whoever he's talking to is browsing the supermarket for parmesan.

"Still living with your ex and his partner?"

Jack slowly tucks his phone away. His eyes track mine carefully. "Still hunting for the right project."

I'm tempted to admit that he was right about renovating and ask for help, but I don't know how to ask. Don't know if I should, either.

I sink into banter that I usually reserve for Milo and Talia. For a moment, I'm not a failing caregiver. I'm just a guy chatting to another guy.

It's refreshing.

The line moves at a snail's pace, and at this rate, I'm not getting five minutes to shower let alone twenty.

He leaves his cart, views the meat counter, and steps back beside me. The air throbs in the few inches between us. Maybe that hot shower will have to be a cold one.

He peers into my cart. "I hope this isn't a representation of what stocks your fridge."

"I make a mean"—I lean over and check the frozen meal —"lasagna. Am pretty good with the two-minute noodles, too."

"Your diet sounds frightening."

"Frighteningly yummy."

Genuinely horrified, he says, "Throw something green in there, Christ."

"Wasabi?"

He curls a fist around the handle of my cart. His hand is large with squarish knuckles and blunt fingernails. He adjusts his grip and his pinkie brushes mine. The friction of his tough-ened skin sends blood rushing to my dick.

He steers me out of line toward the fresh produce section. "Go."

I act affronted, but my grin slips through. "You owe me sausage."

He rolls forward in line, gaze fixed on me. We talked about Milo's love of chicken and peas, so he knows what I'm standing in line for. "How much would you like?"

"Three kilos," I say, rolling toward the veggies.

"That's a lot of meat."

I glance back at him over my shoulder. "Well, it's the only meat I'm getting, so."

His arched brow follows me to the zucchini. It follows me later, too.

Not to the shower—I have a run-in with a wall of tuna cans and end up five minutes late to pick up Milo—but much later, to bed, where I curl a slicked palm around my aching cock and attempt to pump out the pressures of life.

Chapter Eight

JACK

I HIKE ACROSS THE EMPTY TENNIS AND NETBALL COURTS toward the back of school and my reliable truck. My foot buzzes numbly since it fell asleep during a painfully long staff meeting.

Now to shuttle my ass across town to Karori. Howie, the current owner of my dream home, asked me to afternoon tea. Butterflies have been wildly dancing in my gut since the call. Maybe he's ready to talk numbers.

Through the chain-link fence separating the courts from the cul-del-sac, I spot Milo rummaging through his school bag. He withdraws something black.

Milo is the only kid here—and no wonder. It's almost half past three.

I approach him. Concern ticks in my belly that he's still here, alone. "Waiting out here for your brother?"

"Hey, Mr. Woodpecker. He'll be here soon."

"Sure he's not parked out the front of school?"

Milo emphatically shakes his head. "He *only* parks out here now."

My gaze flickers to the parking spot where I found Ben bent over the innards of his car. Only out here? That's . . . interesting.

I probably shouldn't read into that. Or smile.

Nevertheless, I'm doing both.

My gaze snags on a pair of binoculars hanging around Milo's collar. What does he need those for? I scan the cul-de-sac, a standard inner-city street with houses boasting the fashion of the fifties, and the school's netball courts at the end.

Nothing particularly binocular-worthy.

The magnolias punctuating the sidewalk are pretty, but easy to appreciate without lenses.

"Binoculars?" I ask.

"'Bonding time' with Ben." He makes a face as though the idea is stupid, but he can't hold it and a grin shines through.

"Bonding time?" Connecting with his brother is a good plan, but I'm a little skeptical about the binoculars.

"It's our common interest." Milo swings his binoculars like a pendulum. "We take these around the neighborhood and look into people's yards."

I blink, and blink again. W*hat?*

"Want to look? There's two going at it in that garden." Milo lifts the binoculars.

Christ.

Maybe Ben is struggling with this gig more than I thought.

I gently urge the binoculars down. "Peeping into people's yards is an invasion of privacy."

"We never sneak onto their property. Why make yards pretty if we can't look at them?"

"Not with binoculars."

"But the details are better up close and personal."

Tires churr over the road, and Ben's hatchback slides into a free slot with a friendly honk. Ben spills out, along with an empty bottle. He swears, and chases it down the street.

"Fuck, I'm late," he calls. "This day, I tell you. Made the mistake of drinking a liter of Fanta before I left and got stuck in the Victoria tunnel. Traffic's a nightmare. My bladder is about to burst."

He snatches the bottle and tosses it into the car. His posture straightens when he notices me. He stuffs his thumbs into his insanely tight jeans, and an undeniable swagger seeps into his step.

I'm thrown back to our moment at the supermarket almost a week ago. A flirtatious dimple deepens one side of his mouth and disappears when he drags his focus on his brother. "Shit. Binoculars. I left mine at home."

Milo shrugs. "We can take turns using mine."

"You hog them."

"Only if the view's worthwhile."

Ben closes the gap. A frigid breeze combs through his hair and hits my face, but Ben's body buffers it from the rest of me.

Milo peers through the binoculars and pulls the strap from around his neck. "Take a look. Toward the kowhai tree."

Ben lifts, looks, and laughs. "Boisterous. That energy!"

"Those two really going at it, huh?"

"Mmm. Bit early to be going at it though—"

"Or really late."

Jesus Christ. Rather laissez-faire about the whole Peeping Tom act, aren't they? I step in front of Ben, blocking his view. Howie will have to wait. I gotta have a word with this guy.

He pries the binoculars from his nose and smirks at me. "Warn a man, would you?"

"Ben, I can open the staff bathroom for you." I need to address this, but not in front of Milo.

Relief floods Ben's face. "Thanks." He fishes out his car

keys and throws them to Milo. "I'll be back in ten. There's Fanta in the glove box."

He extends the binoculars, and I confiscate them before striding toward the school.

Ben jostles to keep up beside me. "So, Jack. We meet again."

I throw him a knowing look. "Funny that."

I don't approach the peeping conversation until Ben's finished in the gym bathroom and I've locked back up.

I rest against the concrete block, gripping the binoculars. The quad stretches behind him as sunlight plays peek-a-boo with the clouds. Our intermittent, elongated shadows almost touch but not quite.

Ben gestures for the binoculars, and I loop the strap around my neck. "Ben, mate, I don't think this is the best 'bonding' you could be doing with your brother."

He drops his arm. "Why not? It's fun. And those birds were really going at it."

"This is what I'm—wait." His words catch up to me. "Birds as in . . . the term for sexualizing females?"

Ben's voice squeaks. "As in birds. As in feathers and beaks. As in tui, native to the country."

"Tui?" Not two going at it. *Tui* going at it.

Ben stares at me, studying my relief. A flush creeps up his neck and he rocks on his heels indignantly. "No way."

"Ben—"

"I am not a Peeping Tom!" He pauses and adds, "And if I were, I wouldn't be peeping at 'birds.' But I'm not, and wouldn't. Ever."

"I've made an ass of myself."

"You sure have."

I hand over the binoculars. "My apologies."

His gaze sparks and he sets his hands on his hips. There's something almost gleeful in the way he leans toward me.

"Sorry is a verb, Mr. Pecker." That spark in his eyes brightens, and his smile glints with mischief.

I'm not sure I should ask.

But I'm going to. "A verb?"

"If you want to apologize, how about you do it by helping me?"

My stomach kicks with anticipation. I shouldn't want to know what he means so badly, but I do. "Help you out with what?"

Ben curls his hand around my arm and urges me toward our vehicles. He tells me to follow him in my truck, and despite my meeting with Howie, I do.

Five minutes later, I meet a wildly grinning Ben on the sidewalk in front of his place.

Milo hoofs out of sight. A fresh gust wallops us. It smells like rain and coming to a crossroads.

Ben hands me the binoculars, his voice spirited. "Take a good peep, and we'll talk about how badly it needs doing."

I swallow a smirk at the double-entendre. Looks like there's another conversation we need to have. I keep my voice even. "I'll need to check inside, too."

He passes over his keys. "Go nuts."

This guy is going to kill me. "You're not coming?"

He drops the subtext. A small shudder ripples through him before he slicks on a smile. "I'll wait in the guest cottage."

I enter the house and breathe in a lungful of stale air. Dust layers the furniture in every room. It's like walking into a museum of crammed bookshelves and sports equipment. Oriental rugs curled at the edges stretch over hardwood floors.

Only the master bedroom remains bare.

I swallow a sympathetic ache.

I type a few notes on my phone and head toward the cottage. The laundry room tastes fresh. At least the boys venture this close to the main house.

Ben is sitting on the raised veranda to the guest cottage, legs over the side, feet kicking anxiously through the long grass.

He spots me and stands. He slicks on a cocky smile. "Needs a lot of hard work, huh?"

Not five seconds in his company, and the air charges with a fiery static. It reminds me how long it's been since someone has flirted with me and admired me with blatant lust.

How long it's been since I've responded this strongly to it.

"Depends on the modifications you want to do." I tell him what needs doing as far as I can tell after twenty minutes. It's time to pull back, suggest a few good contractors, and meet Howie.

Bloody hell. His raking gaze rushes right to my cock, and I'm battling images of pushing Ben against the patio pillar and crushing my lips against his. Battling images of reaching into his jeans, taking his hot, hard dick in my hand and watching his flush spread to his cheeks as he gasps and spills his seed. I'm battling images of him sinking his weight against me with a string of curses about how fucking hard he came.

Jesus. I need to rip myself back to the truck.

I step back, stuffing my hands in my pockets.

Disappointment flitters over his face, but he rolls it off like he expected it. "You need a project, I have one. What do you say?"

"Not a great idea."

"Why not?"

"You're smarter than that."

He opens his mouth and closes it, and combs a hand through all the delightful ginger hair.

"That obvious I fancy you, huh?"

Not just from the word-porn in front of the house. Or the way his eyes travel up and down my length. "You ran into a wall of tuna cans at the supermarket while watching me."

He presses his lips together. "You owed me meat, and I wanted to show you my zucchini."

"You were scoping out the guy I was talking to."

Ben throws up his hands. "I thought he was robbing you."

"Of fresh produce?"

"Who was he?"

"My ex, Luke." I lean in, chuckling. "That scowl further proves my point, Ben."

He crosses his arms. "Fine! I'm attracted to you." He mutters, "Definitely only physically."

Smartass.

"I can't get involved with parents from school." He's about to retort so I cut him off with an amused laugh. "Or brothers."

"Ah, dammit. Worth a shot."

A shot I can't let him score.

I ABSORB THE BEAUTIFUL TIMBER BONES OF THE VILLA DINING room. Light pours over the rimu dining table from the skylights and the sash windows.

I sigh and sip the warm lavender tea Howie made for us.

He chuckles from across the table, shaking his head. Age sags the skin at his eyes and flecks the backs of his trembling hands. His voice is husky. "You're imagining what you'll do with the place, aren't you?"

His physical health might not be what it was, but his mind is sharp. I pour him more tea. "Guilty."

"I like you, Jack. Straightforward and solid. Just like my niece keeps reminding me."

His niece is Kresley's principal, Stephanie Ryan. Thanks to her, I discovered this jewel during a Christmas barbecue she hosted.

I lean in, catching his eye. "Don't keep me hanging in suspense here. Are you selling?"

"Soon, boy. Soon."

"You'll sell to me, right?" A note of desperation fractures my voice, but I temper it with a grin.

"I'll sell to who wants it the most."

"Definitely me, then."

He studies me over the rim of his china cup. "We've been meeting over tea for, let's see, eight years now?"

"Eight years and five months."

"You still haven't found a partner. Grown a family."

The punch is painful, and I sink back in my chair. "Rather straightforward yourself."

"Forgive me, Jack. I've lived long enough to encounter many men in my life, and I agree with my niece, you are among the best of them. I wish you happiness."

I acknowledge his apology with a nod. "This villa will make me happy."

"They do say home is where the heart is."

"Mine's here."

He smiles sadly. "It's unlikely before summer, but when I'm ready to move, I'll let you know."

Chapter Nine

JACK

CHRIST.

I shove a pillow over my head and wish the next fifteen minutes were over. Every night, it's the same. The smacking against the wall, the vibrations humming through my headboard, the gasping as my ex fucks his lover.

Awkward doesn't begin to describe it.

It's also arousing, dammit. Shouldn't I be more morally grounded at thirty-nine?

Quickened moaning has me squeezing the pillow at my ears. My hardon is painful, and worse is the loneliness jacking through me.

It's been so long since I've woken up with a man I cared for.

So long, since I've woken with a family.

So long, since I've said the words "I love you."

The headboard rattles, the groaning peaks, and my dick throbs like a son-of-a-bitch.

Sam is Luke's heart now. They're happy, and I'm happy for them.

But for the love of God, I need to move out.

❧

WHEN THEY START FUCKING AGAIN AT SIX THE NEXT MORNING, I throw myself into jogging gear and hit the leaf-slickened streets.

I fork toward Berhampore. The remodeling job Ben offered has been plaguing my mind. Especially since Howie won't sell before summer.

The McCormick bungalow could be the perfect interim project.

Could be, if not for that one small problem . . .

The McCormick backyard sits on the fringe of the town belt, and I jog over packed dirt and pine-needles. My step crushes the tannins and spices the air.

"Jack?"

I halt to a sliding stop. Getting caught hadn't been part of the plan. I counted on the boys being in bed this early in the morning as I gawk at their house and contemplate what a fool I'd be for taking the job.

With a grimace, I turn toward Ben's voice, scanning over trees and backyards.

"Over here." Ben's figure slides down the trunk of a bushy pohutakawa.

Bark shavings stick to his jeans and the form-fitting polar fleece he has zipped up his neck. He dusts himself off, binoculars jiggling from his neck.

I roll a forearm over the sweat beading at my forehead and cross to him. "Morning. You're up already?"

Circles shadow his eyes, but his mouth lifts in a spirited smile. "The early bird catches the worm."

"Literally," Milo softly calls from above me.

I jerk my head up. A few branches above, a pair of legs dangles.

I stage whisper to Ben, "Does that kid ever have his feet on the ground outside school?"

"There's a kākā up here!"

Air stirs as Ben presses the warmed rubber of his binoculars against my eyes. "Check it out."

"What am I looking for?"

"Beauty, Jack."

I steer the binoculars in his direction and his smile magnifies. "A little more direction-specific, please."

Laughing, Ben crowds close and raises a hand, pointing above Milo. "A young one. Such scarlet plumage!"

"And that's coming from *Ben*," Milo says drolly.

Ben good-naturedly casts a hand through his tousled red hair.

The bird picks at something in the tree trunk. Sap, perhaps. "Looks like a kea."

Both boys go unusually quiet. "What?"

I pull down the binoculars to find Ben shaking his head. "You're not as all-knowing as I thought."

I bark out a laugh and return the binoculars. "You give me far too much credit."

"Do you always jog this way?" Ben asks curiously.

He's got me. "No."

"So why are you here?"

I gesture toward his backyard, fifty meters down the path. "Did you call the contractors I suggested?"

"All booked. We can either wait, or sell without changes and hope for a decent price." Hopefulness glints in his clever eye.

Milo tosses a twig at Ben and he spins away from it, lurching his body toward mine. He stops a breath from me, his gentle freshly-soaped scent hitting my nose. He cups his mouth and yells treeward. "What was that for?"

"We're not selling. Mr. Pecker. Please fix it until he likes our home again?"

They have a project, and I need one.

I dart a glance to Milo and back.

A wind whistles through the trees. The scent of pine washes over us. Streaks of morning light sift through the branches, streaking the carpet of pinecones, tree trunks, and Ben's brilliant hair. Flecks of gold shimmer over his jaw as his dark eyes meet mine expectantly.

I don't say the words.

They're pulled from me.

"I'll do it." I rub my jaw and tell myself again it will be fine. "I'll remodel in return for free rent. You'll provide the funds for materials."

Ben's posture sharpens. "You will?"

"But these projects aren't done overnight . . ."

"You'll need time, I understand."

"Maybe six months? I'd like to live in the house first. Develop a better sense of its potential." I snag his gaze. "I'm not the type to rush into things without proper consideration."

He's shrewd. As my words sink in, he smirks. "I'm totally the type. It's definitely a flaw."

It might be a blazing omen of how tricky this year will get —but I made the boundaries clear. I'd never act on any fleeting impulses.

I ignore the unsettled lurch in my stomach.

Chapter Ten

JACK

I FIDDLE WITH MY COLLAR FOR THE THIRD TIME OVER A breakfast of scrambled eggs. I'm not used to the dress shirt, and it's not my favorite choice.

Luke waltzes into the dining room, yawning. I point my fork toward the kitchen. "Eggs are in the oven. Coffee on the pot. Top me up, while you're at it."

Making breakfast is usually just that: making breakfast. Today, though, it's designed to put the boys in a good mood. I'm informing them I'm outta here and they gotta spend this Saturday helping me haul my shit to the Berhampore bungalow.

Luke carries the coffeepot over, drops into the seat next to me, and digs into my eggs.

"Lazy ass." I grin at him.

"Usually I'm energetic in the morning. I'm getting old."

"Or not getting enough sleep, hmm?"

The fork pauses at his lips. "We keeping you up?"

"Let's just say, you helped me jump into a rather . . . challenging project."

"You're moving out?"

"Yeah."

Luke nods and eats more of my eggs. "Hard project, is it?"

"You could say that."

I pile eggs on a plate for him. He takes it with a gracious smile. "These are delicious." He eyes my shirt. "You look different today."

"Different? Give me my eggs back."

He protects his plate. "Back off. I meant different good."

"I think you mean different *very* good," Sam says, joining us. "What's the occasion?"

Luke answers for me, because he knows this is my only dress shirt. I only wear it twice a year. "Feedback from teacher evaluations. But I don't know why you bother with the shirt. Principal Ryan is more interested in acting professional than looking the part."

"You make an excellent point. Wait right here."

Sam grips my arm. "Leave it on."

Luke gets up and draws Sam into a kiss. "Want some eggs?"

I'm already on it. They're still murmuring between kisses when I return with a plate and coffee for Sam. The tenderness echoes around me, making me painfully aware how long it has been since I've felt that. I've had plenty of sex—I'm not a monk—but little intimacy.

Nothing since, well, Luke.

Luke catches me staring and his expression softens.

I slide the plate onto Sam's spot and bury myself in tangy coffee. "Carpool today?" Our schedules don't often allow for it, but when they do, we try to save on exhaust fumes.

"Nah. Gotta drive to Lower Hutt after we wrap up classes today. Jeremy booked indoor soccer."

I lift a brow. "Indoor?"

Sam groans. "For my benefit. The balls are soft."

Luke's eyes glitter with amusement. "Your son loves you, Sam."

"Loves to make fun of me, you mean."

They share a secret smile, and an ache flares in my chest. It's not just the intimacy that snags me, it's the air. When it was just me, the place tasted like wood, paint, and polish. Now it smells of Luke's cooking, herbal shower gels and aftershaves, dust from their combined book collection, and sweat from the home gym. The rooms are warmer. Less echo.

Every breath feels like family, and it picks at a tender wound.

I grab my wallet and keys. "Have fun at soccer, Sam." I nod toward Luke. "Catch you at work. And save your strength tonight."

Luke chokes on a forkful of eggs.

"Save our strength?" Sam asks.

"You two are helping me move my shit tomorrow."

I sit in a frayed fabric chair opposite Principal Ryan as she reviews her notes with a friendly smile. She wears a blazer with a casual T-shirt that promotes breast cancer awareness.

"I think we're done with the business side of things," she says, and her shoulders relax. "I hear you visited Uncle Howie. You're almost up there as much as I am."

We share a laugh.

"I keep putting in good words for you."

I thank her. "I've taken on a small renovation project in the meantime."

"Where do you get the energy, Jack?"

"The benefits of a thirty-hour work week." I hesitate. "Look, the project is Milo McCormick's family home. I'm helping them whip the house into shape before they sell."

She nods slowly. "The McCormicks. Two boys I'll never forget." She shakes her head. "That Benjamin spent every other week in my office. Now, Milo does."

I roll my shoulders. "I wanted to be upfront about working with a student's caregiver."

"It's not the first time you've helped parents before. You've certainly been an asset to the community." A slight warning glazes her eye. "This shouldn't be any different."

I read the subtext. *Keep it as professional as always.*

"Of course."

"That's settled then." She stands. "Mrs. Devon is coming now. Wish me luck I can carve out a lunchbreak. She loves to gossip."

All I hear is a warning not to do anything stupid or Mrs. Devon will find out and there goes my villa.

Chapter Eleven

BEN

MEN HAVE BEEN LOADING THE MAIN HOUSE WITH JACK'S belongings all morning. Thank God I had the excuse of taking Milo to our counselling session.

I watch from my parked car across the road as two guys and a teenager wave to Jack on their way out the gate.

Milo is too buried in his phone and chatting with his mate to recognize we arrived home.

I stare at Jack on the verandah dragging in the last of his boxes. It's a dry day and sunlight settles over the wild lawn and glares off the bay windows. Jack grabs a box, his back slipping into a wedge of light.

Throwing keys at him and telling him to go nuts wasn't the friendliest greeting. I should welcome him properly. Maybe show him the trick to re-opening the bathroom lock.

But, fuck. Can I go inside?

I wring the steering wheel, and Milo jerks his head up.

"Oh, we're home."

He opens his belt.

"How much for you to show Jack how to jimmy the bathroom lock?" I ask.

"A hundred bucks."

"Are you out of your mind? Ten."

Determination sets in his jaw. "A thousand bucks."

"That's not how negotiation works."

"Yeah, it is. I want you to go inside again."

He storms across the road and speaks to Jack before he rounds the side of the house. Jack spots me cowering in my car.

Okay.

So what, every time I've walked inside the last year I've started hyperventilating?

I've got this.

I wave, tell myself to stop being an idiot, and pull myself to Jack. The veranda groans underfoot much the same as I do inside.

Jack dusts his hands, and smiles. Dark canvas pants stretch across his hips, falling loose down his leg and bunching at his boots. The sleeves of his tomato red T-shirt are shoved up to his elbows, and the hem has flicked up to his navel, showing off tan skin and a smattering of dark hair.

"Milo says you want to show me something inside?"

My gaze jerks to the shadowy interior. "Yeah. There's a trick to the toilet lock."

We step inside. Through the first door is a narrow conservatory filled with ladders and tools. Jack watches me take it in. I shove my shaky hands into my pockets and slant him a smirk. "Some mean décor happening in here."

"You should see the bedroom. All boxes."

We walk deeper into the house and I peer into each room. "You have more things than I thought you would."

"Is that a problem?"

I shake my head. "I imagined you as a wanderer. Just the clothes on your back and your tools."

"Not a collector of antique furniture?"

"I should have guessed."

"I am a carpenter."

"And old."

Jack laughs, an unexpected reprieve from the weight of walking in here.

We arrive at the bathroom. There's a tiled tub, a cabinet shower, a basin, and a door leading to the toilet.

I herd him into the toilet and shut the door. There's barely a foot between us as I lock us in. The hairs on my neck lift at the gentle stirring of his breath, and my spine tickles with a shiver at Jack's solid frame walling me—even though he's keeping as much distance as possible.

A tiny stained-glass window and a burgundy lampshade over the bulb cast a suggestive atmosphere.

The ache of being inside the house again clashes with the ache of feeling a man in sudden proximity.

"Y-you have to lift the frame of the door and jiggle the key right and then left to unlock." I show him, and fuck it up. My nervous laugh flutters around us. "How smooth."

I try again, flustered, and Jack's fingers knock mine as he pinches the key. "Let me try."

I sink against the wall in embarrassment as Jack smoothly unlocks the door.

He steps out and I burst past him.

Jack remains unruffled, face schooled of emotion.

"So, yeah. Welcome. Just a heads up, sometimes Milo wanders in here. He gets nostalgic, and I . . ." Can't easily come in after him.

"That's okay."

"Right. Otherwise, this is your space and you won't be bothered. Actually, small caveat. We share a laundry room.

The guest cottage only has space for a washing machine or a dishwasher—and let's just say it wasn't Sophie's choice."

We walk back through the house and I freeze outside my parents' room. Hardwood floors and violet, floral wallpaper punch me with memories.

"Ben?"

"Yup?"

"You okay?"

I wheeze. "It's, ah, I don't usually venture so far into the house."

"I'm sorry, mate."

"The sooner we sell the better."

I retreat to the living room and Jack's belongings, absorbing the mix of old furniture: the armchairs I grew up with and Jack's wooden coffee table and carved lampstand.

Jack leans against the doorjamb and eyes me carefully. He wants to ask questions. Thing is I can't talk about it.

If I do, I may cry, and I've spent months hiding my tears. From anyone.

Even from Milo, and I trust him the most.

I laser-focus on the cracked stained-glass window, a reminder of the anger that followed me into this house directly after their deaths, when I removed all their belongings.

Talia had been there and made three trips to the Salvation Army.

A truck picked up the rest. Their bed, the armoire, and Mum's favorite rocking chair.

Milo's and my room are the same as before, minus some clothing.

I suppose Jack has his boxes in my old room.

Good thing. It'll ensure I never get cocky enough to go in there. Not that he's receptive to that.

I cock him a grin. "If you need anything, you know where we are."

Chapter Twelve

BEN

A PILE OF DIRTY CLOTHES GROWS AT MY FEET, WHERE I'M standing in the kitchen hugging a laundry bag. I had asked if there was *something* Milo needed washing, not everything from the past year.

The pile forms a moat around my ankles, and is still growing.

Shorts, socks, and undershirts.

Finally the clothes stop sling-shotting from Milo's room. "Sure you're not forgetting anything?" I ask sarcastically.

A T-shirt flies and hits me against the throat. The unpleasant whiff has me dropping it like a hot potato.

Milo strolls into the kitchen pulling binoculars over his head.

I lunge for his arm as he slides toward the front door. "Hold it. I can't carry this alone."

He reluctantly helps me trundle it to the laundry at the back of the main house.

I open the machine and start stuffing it with Milo's clothes. "Decision. You only need three T-shirts. One on, one in the wash, one in case this gets wet."

"Three is a stingy number."

"Not when you're the one doing the washing." I pull myself out of the washing machine and eye Milo closely. He notices and starts to sidle away. "Wait. You're eleven. I started doing the washing at twelve. I remember, because it was mostly your shitty nappies—"

He squeaks. "Three T-shirts are good. In fact, two are fine as well."

An amused chuckle carries over the deck and we both swing toward Jack. He's rocking jeans and a flannel shirt, and his hair is damp and disheveled. He's carrying a basket of laundry.

Two weeks have passed since Jack moved into the main house, and we've barely seen each other.

I've admired his sweaty body as he tugged vines off the house, we've traded friendly waves en route to our vehicles, and Milo's pissed him off a couple times—something Jack deals with well. He quickly and firmly puts my bucko in place.

It's admirable what a commanding voice can do.

But this is the first time he's approached us.

"Three T-shirts are fine," Jack muses, "as long as you don't plan on mud-surfing like your brother seems fond of."

His gaze hits me with a gust of giddiness.

I lean back against the machine. "Heard all that, did you?"

"I approve of Milo helping. I think seven T-shirts is better though. One on, six in the wash. One load per week."

Milo slinks out of sight, probably hoping I'll forget to make him do the laundry. Fat chance. I'll yell at him until I'm blue, then guiltily give in and wash it myself.

Jack settles his basket on a bench. "Seven pairs of socks work, too."

"You seem oddly fond of the number." I eye him suspiciously. "Show me your underwear." I reach out and cheekily grab him by the beltloops.

He lifts an eyebrow.

"They're day of the week ones, aren't they?"

Jack slides past me. The air shifts with his scent and I shatter into goosebumps.

"You don't give up, do you?"

He reaches for the laundry detergent. "One of my better traits. Besides, have you looked in the mirror lately?"

"Damn, Ben—" His voice is firm and frustrated.

I lean against the dryer beside him. He's taken over pouring soap into the machine and setting it on a cold wash. My belly cinches at the sight of a manly guy being domestic. It screams protection and comfort, and the cave dweller in me approves.

Which is about the only thing that approves this pesky attraction. "I get it, Jack." I say quietly. "It's not going any further than flirting."

He side-eyes me. "Maybe we should leave the flirting, too."

I give him my blankest stare. "Meet me halfway, here."

His lips jump at the edges. "I'm Milo's teacher."

"This adult stuff sucks."

Jack erupts on a laugh and quickly reins it in. "Tell me about it."

Water gushes into the machine and I sigh. "You're hot, you're strong, and—other than your painful ignorance on native birds—you're smart. All reasons I'm attracted. And you're *right there*, and I gotta say, the convenience makes you ten percent hotter."

Jack snorts and gathers an armful of Milo's clothes and sets them on the bench. "Stay honest, Ben."

"You're right. I should get out there. Hell, I'm mostly carpal tunnel at this point."

Jack shuts his eyes briefly. "I hear a 'but'."

"*Getting* butt is impossible with work and Milo. I don't dare hire a babysitter after the roof incident—"

I'm cut off by a shrill scream, and my heart pumps its way into my throat. "Milo?"

I dash across the weedy yard to the back of the house.

Milo is calling my name, voice panicked. I scrape my hand on the corrugated iron gate in my rush to find him.

"Ben," he calls again. I shoot over tree roots to my brother wobbling to his feet at the base of a pine.

I hear Jack crunching right behind me. Hear him swear at the same time I do.

Blood sluices down Milo's face and the hand that's pressed over a wound at his temple.

"Oh fuck. Oh fuck. Oh fuck." I pull Milo into my shaking arms.

Milo groans and shifts his hand. His skin has split open an inch and I see something white. Fuck, I see his skull.

"Oh fuck. He's dying. I've killed him." *Mum and Dad left me one job.*

"You haven't killed him," Jack says steadily.

He scoops Milo out of my arm and lifts him up. "Apply pressure to the cut," he tells Milo as he strides toward the street. "Ben, we'll take my truck to the hospital."

I don't stop my 'oh fuck' mantra until we reach his vehicle.

"Grab the keys from my pocket and open the door."

Jack's arms flex under Milo's weight. The effort is beginning to pinch.

I dive a hand into Jack's tight pocket and get stuck drawing out his keys.

"Look at me," Jack says, demanding I pay attention.

I lift my eyes, glancing once to Milo's head.

Jack is all calm authority. "It's a small cut. Nothing a few stitches won't fix."

"Stitches," I repeat, nodding stupidly.

"Now breathe and slowly pull out the keys."

I do as he says. Jack steers me with step-by-step instructions, and I follow them. I sling myself in the passenger side and help pull Milo in over the front seat. I rest Milo's head on my thigh, and Jack has Milo's legs bent at his chest.

Milo finds my hand and squeezes. "I'll be fine, Ben."

"Course you will, bucko. Course you will."

There have been few truly important people in my life. Mum. Dad. Milo. And Talia.

That's it.

It's not as though I shun potential connections, it's simply that these connections are rare.

I don't know what makes a person important, exactly. Sharing basic principles and experiences are great adhesives, but it's more than that. Like, even in silences, I feel comfortable with my best friend. Even in the middle of a heated disagreement, I feel safe with my brother.

It sounds insane, but it's like our auras bond.

Jack isn't one of these important people.

Hardly. I barely know him.

But when he reassuringly pats Milo's knees and starts the truck, my heart clenches.

Like, he *could* be.

At the hospital, a doctor takes Milo right away.

We follow, and the adrenalin of the moment catches up to me. I haul in a lungful of air. Jack curls an arm around my back and gently tugs me toward a chair. The heat of his palm oozes against my shoulder blade.

I blink in the shiny floors, the blood sluicing over Milo's face, and Jack, there at my side. His fingers drift to the small of my back and settle snugly. "Come," he says, applying pressure.

"I can never let him out of my sight. Not for a single minute." I halt, horror slamming into me. "I'm never getting laid again."

The doctor's head jerks up. Milo groans and mumbles about checking if we are truly related. Jack suppresses his amusement as he guides me to a seat.

I shuffle low into my seat, unable to look away from the doctor sewing stitches into my brother's temple.

"I have an idea," Jack says quietly, and I peer up at his contemplative face. "I'll look after Milo on Friday nights."

I grip his solid knee as I push up and look at him. His muscles under my palm jump and I reluctantly drag my fingers off him. "Why?"

"I had my twenties, and you should exploit yours. Take a break from playing parent."

"I can't ask that of you."

"I'm across the yard. We're talking a few hours a week. More importantly, Milo can't frighten me off."

I snort. "You gotta give me some tips."

Jack's chuckle soothes my nerves.

Milo grins once the gauze is taped over his wound. His face has been wiped clean, but his clothes are soaked with blood.

"At least this experience has taught us something," Jack murmurs.

"Not to climb trees?" Milo says dispirited.

Jack shakes his head. "You definitely need a minimum of three T-shirts."

Chapter Thirteen

BEN

I WANT TO BE PRESSED AGAINST A WALL——ANY WALL——AND HAVE my brains fucked out.

It's a typical mid-winter Friday a couple of weeks after school holidays. I'm sitting in a dully lit bar watching rain drizzle down the window, waiting for my Grindr hookup to arrive.

Since taking up Jack's offer to babysit, Fridays have become date nights.

It's been six weeks, and I've gone out with four guys. None of them ended up in my bed—or rather, theirs. I'm not messing with Milo's head like that by having strangers over for conjugal visits.

Jack always grins, carefully avoiding taking in my outfit. With a tiny flicker in his eye, he wishes me a good—and safe— night out, and hurriedly pulls Monopoly or Scrabble off the shelf.

I can't lie. This little look of his follows me out most Fridays.

It's distracting as fuck, and I spend most of my dates wondering what Jack is thinking behind his carefully guarded expressions.

It's what I'm doing now.

My phone leaps to life, and I'm greeted with a hungover picture of Talia and a roguish-looking dude twice her height.

Talia: Why do I always fall for gay guys? LOL.

Ben: You should come home and be a magnet for me.

Talia: You do fine on your own.

Ben: I'm waiting for a date now, and all I can think about is Jack and Milo at home. I have a problem.

Talia: Many, Ben.

Ben: Haha. True though.

Talia: Another five months, and I'll be the annoying buzz in your ear again.

Ben: You mean my conscience.

Talia: You got it.

My hookup "Felix" waltzes through the front door wearing a casual blazer and bow tie, stylish hair, and a cheerful grin.

I stuff thoughts of Jack as deep as I can. Jack can't fuck me. Felix can.

My hookup spots me, and heads toward the window seats I scored.

Goal: get fucked.

First step: Give this guy a chance.

He closes the distance with a spring in his step and halts.

He has a casual grace and an attractive full-of-life presence. Not as tall or as muscular as Jack, though. And there's a flicker of hesitation in his eyes when he sits.

Similar to the hesitation I see every day with Jack.

I sit forward and clasp my fingers together. "Felix, right?"

Dark tendrils of hair curl over his forehead. He has striking eyes and a soothing voice. "Ben. Nice to meet you." I shake his hand. It's an oddly formal move that I don't expect from a guy in his early twenties. I like it, though. It seems like something Jack might do—

I shove that thought away. *Give the guy a chance.*

"Can I get you a beer?"

"I can't do this!" he blurts and lurches to his feet. "I'm sorry. Maybe I'm not gay or bisexual after all."

Oh, okay. "Felix?"

Panicked, he laughs. I see myself mirrored in him and my chest twists. I stand. "Felix. How about a friendly beer? Nothing else?"

Slowly, he nods.

Over a lager, he apologizes again. "I just thought maybe . . . But I don't feel anything. I'm sorry to lead you on like this."

My sigh ripples the surface of my beer. "It probably wouldn't have happened anyway. I can't seem to commit to any hookup lately."

My phone buzzes.

Jack: Milo snuck out his window. Found him in the main house. He doesn't want to head back, I let him hang out in his old room.

I slide from my stool. "Um, sorry, Felix. My brother needs me."

"No worries. I'm familiar with the job of big brother. Have four siblings—three younger."

"Jesus. I can barely manage one."

He laughs. With a wave, I skip out the door into the frigid night. It's a fifteen-minute hike home, but I do it in ten.

Outside the back of the house, I nervously shuffle over the deck. *Get over it, Ben.*

I steal inside.

The stained-glass window has been repaired; the laundry and bathrooms have been retiled and had new sinks installed.

Three windows now have double-pane glass. And my bank account has a nice little dent in it.

I pause outside the lounge where Jack is relaxing on an armchair. A lamp glows over him and the book he's reading. It's a warm picture, but it's also a lonely one.

I guess he hadn't heard me announce myself. "Jack?" I knock on the doorframe.

His book hits the side table. His open shirt flaps as he crosses his arms against his wide chest. His smile is cautious like all the smiles he's been slanting me the last weeks.

So much for forgetting about Jack's indecipherable glances.

"Ben. You're back."

I enter the room, floorboards groaning in the quickly electrifying space.

"I didn't mean for you to run home," he says.

"Well, I wasn't sure . . . Is he okay? Where is he?"

"Asleep in his bed."

Oh. Right. Not crying in a corner or throwing a tantrum. I suppose I could have called.

I suppose I wanted the excuse to come home.

I drift toward an adjacent armchair. I want to grab Milo and hurry back to the cottage, but I need my post-date chat with Jack.

It's become tradition.

Usually I arrive at the guest cottage after my failed date and find Jack at our two-person table working on designs for the main house. Milo would be long in bed, and instead of letting Jack go on his way, I'd take out beer from the fridge, hand him a bottle, and ask questions.

I want that tonight, too.

"Can I sit a sec?" I ask.

"It's your house."

"Your living space, though."

"Sit. I'll grab us a drink."

I sit, biting a smile. I think this part of the evening is as important to him as it is to me. "Fanta?"

He snorts. "I will never stock that rot in my fridge."

"I'll run to the cottage then—"

He sends me a baleful look that simply dares me to trot off for the fizzy beverage. It's the most pronounced expression he's had in weeks.

"How about we settle on coffee?"

I'll be wide awake as it is. "Okay."

Jack leaves the room. With him gone, the space yanks at my chest. Milo used to toddle behind this chair and poop on the floor, sending Mum into hysterics while Dad cleaned up.

The good memories pinch most.

I push off the armchair and hunt down Jack. His presence fills the small kitchen, and he acts like he's lived here for years. A weird thought, him knowing my childhood kitchen so well.

"Nearly there," he says, and I breathe in the percolating scent of roasted coffee and impending conversation.

He'll tell me what shenanigans my brother tried on him, and I'll laugh, a small ache twisting in my belly as I wish I could have been a part of it.

Papers stud one side of the counter, and I nosey through rough sketches of kitchen ideas.

Jack pulls two mugs from the overhead cupboard. "I wanted to talk to you about the idea of removing a couple walls and making a great room."

I'm not making sense of the sketches. "With the conservatory? Would that be big enough?"

"Not that wall." He hitches his thumb behind us. "The one adjoining the master bedroom and the living room."

Carving up Mum and Dad's old room?

"The current dining room would make a fantastic master bedroom." Jack pours two coffees. "Only if you feel good about it. But it would increase the value of your house."

For selling.

Because that's what this is all about.

Why Jack is here at all.

I haul in a breath and nod. My voice is scratchy. "Do it."

"I'll work with my architect friend on the schematics and show you some ideas."

I turn around and lean back against the counter like Jack is doing opposite me. He glances over the rim of his cup and takes a sip. "How was your date?"

"Better than last week's. The guy was super nice and super uninterested in me."

Jack nods. "You never mentioned last week's date, was it so bad?"

I hadn't mentioned it because I'd been embarrassed. "All this redness got to him. Brought back fond memories of Garfield."

Jack smirks. "You're joking."

"He thought I should update my Grindr profile. That it's misleading." I pull out my phone, bring up my profile. "What do you think?"

He eyes me carefully before taking my phone and turning off the screen. He hands it back. "He's an idiot if he didn't see how amazing you are."

Heat races up my chest, and I take the phone. Silence magnifies the tickling-shivers.

Jack shifts against the counter. "You could try again if you like. The night is still young."

I shrug and coffee spills, wetting the curve between my thumb and forefinger. I lick it off and catch Jack freeze. His gaze pulls up to mine and he snaps his attention to his coffee.

I pretend to be oblivious, but damn. This teacher thing is so bloody annoying. I want him admitting he thinks about us fucking as often as I do. I want him pulling down my pants, yanking up my T-shirt and knotting my wrists. I want him spinning me around against the cool wall. I want coconut oil slicked into my ass followed by his greedy dick.

I want to return the favor.

Unfortunately, that's not where things stand between us.

I gotta do the adult thing. Channel my growing respect and attraction toward a friendship.

I hope that's what we're starting to have, anyway.

We finish our coffee, and I tiptoe to the kid's old bedroom. His young frame is curled under fauna-and-flora-themed bedcovers. Moonlight washes over his face. The scar at his temple is still prominent.

A badge of my shitty caregiving.

Jack slides next to me. His whisper hits the lobe of my ear. "I'll carry him out back if you want."

"But?"

"But maybe leave him tonight? He's so peaceful."

Jack's right.

It doesn't feel right to disturb him.

I sigh, and our eyes connect. It feels like he can see through me. "You don't mind?"

"Not at all."

We drift through the house to the backdoor. It's time for me to leave, but I don't want to. It's warm around him. The ache of the house wanes when he's nearby.

"What are your plans for the weekend?" I ask, seesawing on the threshold.

"There's an open house tomorrow evening in Eastbourne. I thought I'd check it out. Get inspired."

"Maybe I can come with you?" I clear my voice of its breathiness. "I mean, to learn what to look for when I buy?"

He presses his lips together in consideration. "What about Milo?"

Shit. "He'll come too."

"Are you sure he will?"

"Yeah." One way or another I'll tote Milo there, because I want to see an open house. Want to learn the ins and outs of house-buying.

Want to spend more time developing a friendship with Jack.

~

FOR THE FIRST SATURDAY IN A LONG TIME, I feel on top of the world. I didn't have to work today, and Milo's been in a bright mood since waking up in his old room. His infectious spirit is still going strong this evening as we truck our way around the rocky bays toward Eastbourne.

Jack drives, flannel shirt sleeves rolled up to his elbows. Milo fidgets in the middle between us, his floppy hair peach with the setting sun streaming through the windshield.

I pinch the last piece of Caramello chocolate bar, feeling it squish slightly under the wrapper. I grill Milo. "Which bird likes to follow you in the bush?"

"Fantail!"

"Māori name?"

"Pīwakawaka."

"Follow up question: why does it follow you in the bush?"

Milo rolls his eyes. "It wants the insects that our boots stir up, duh."

"One other fact, and you score the last piece of Caramello bar."

Playing fair? Not in Milo's vocabulary. He bats his puppy-dog eyes and goes in for the kill. "You're my fantail."

Ha! "Because I chase after you all the time?"

"Because Fanta, fantail. It just sounds right."

Aww, I like my brother.

He's the best.

Milo stuffs the chocolate in his mouth as if he didn't just eat three squares.

Jack shakes his head at us. The sunset makes him glow and he's starting to sport a beard. "I have no words for you two."

"Gotta love us, Mr. Woodpecker," Milo squeezes out.

I hook Jack's attention over Milo's head. "We gotta bird-christen the kid. What do you reckon?"

"I'm a Kiwi," Milo says.

"We're all Kiwis," Jack says. "Doesn't count."

I love that Jack takes part so enthusiastically. A keen hop bursts in my veins, and I headlock Milo and give him a noogie. He shrieks and giggles. "You need something more apt—" My gaze flickers toward the street where Jack is slowing down, and I shriek.

"Penguins! At the penguin crossing." Milo takes the words right out of my mouth. "This never happens."

I clutch Milo's arms. "Oh fuck. They're so cute."

Milo leans forward, eyes tracking the tiny birds as they waddle across the road to their nests. "I want to nuzzle my face in their bellies."

"If I haven't nuzzled them all first—"

Jack turns toward us, hand resting on the steering wheel, secret smile simmering in his pinched eyes.

I lift a brow, and he resettles himself, facing forward. He clears his throat. "I suppose I have to get in line if I want to nuzzle?"

A laugh wallops out of me at his unexpected participation in our silliness.

The penguins disappear into the vegetation at the side of the road. Jack rolls his truck forward and takes the last few turns slowly. We park before a playground that's flanked by a coastal café with a wide grassy area and a rocky shoreline.

Dusk shivers over calm seas and layers the world in pink.

Lights twinkle in the bustling café and the chorus of conversations tinkers toward us.

A second car pulls into the parking spot next to ours. Their windows are cracked, and the salty, oily smell of fish 'n' chips makes my mouth water.

"Open house is just up the hill behind us," Jack says across the bonnet.

I cringe, because I haven't quite told Milo why we came out here.

"Open house?" Milo says on cue.

Jack continues, unaware that I used underhand methods to make this trip happen. "It's a nice family home overlooking the sea—"

"No-no-no-no," Milo chants under his breath.

One look at me, and Jack knows. I blush. "Could you get us coffee and a hot chocolate please?"

"No hot chocolate," Milo snaps.

I mouth 'please.'

Jack hesitantly accepts my request. Once he's inside, Milo storms past me and I follow him onto the lumpy grass. The sea stretches behind Milo in tangerine. The hills on the other side of Wellington crown his head. He steers his pouting face toward the playground.

A minute passes, and then, "You told me we're here for the penguins."

"'And stuff'."

"'And stuff' is an ice cream on the beach, not forcing a new home down my throat."

"It's not our new home. I'm learning what to look out for, so when we do buy one, you have a bedroom with a ceiling that doesn't cave in on you."

"I hope it does cave in. I don't want to move."

"Well, we have to eventually."

"So you brought me here under false preteens?"

"*Pretense.*"

"It's my religious belief that older brothers are the worst people to have ever been born."

"Tough luck, bucko."

"I want you to disappear."

"Well, we don't always get what we want."

"Maybe you just need to want it hard enough."

I sigh. I glimpse Jack returning with paper cups in hand. God if I ever needed coffee, it's now. "If I want it really hard, you'll go to bed when I tell you to without me bribing you first?"

"If you want it so bad, you gotta act like it. Do something. Don't get pissy at me because you're a shitty parent."

I rock back with the blow and catch Jack's approaching step stall.

Hurt and embarrassment punch through me.

Milo storms off toward the playground, and I whirl around and kick a lumpy weed. The couple in the car watch me, and my cheeks burn.

Jack sets two coffee cups on a nearby bench. He crosses to me with a down-to-earth gait and clasps my shoulder with a reassuring squeeze. It's more than I deserve.

"Take a seat. Have some coffee."

I plunk my ass down next to him and scoop up a coffee.

The dull white bench is carved with dozens of initials. It's weighted with past romances and the promise of future ones. I rub my thumb over the carved letters between Jack and me. W+S 4EVA. T+G. P+K. How many of them are still in love? Married?

Have children that break their heart?

Milo's figure is silhouetted atop the slide, knees bent, head bowed.

"Well. Fair to say I fucked that one up." I sip the coffee. "Thanks for this, by the way."

"Raising a kid is not easy."

I chuckle and check the fitting of the cup lid. "Kids say stupid, hurtful stuff. I shouldn't have snapped like I did."

"Yeah, kids say shitty things they don't mean and that's allowed. All part of growing up. Parents snap and say things they wish they hadn't, either. All part of parenting."

I gush with relief and gratitude. "How do I measure if I'm doing okay?"

His weight sways toward me and our shoulders bump. Nice and solid, and I wish he would stay there. "I don't know. Pick a small Milo-related goal and see that through?"

I stare at my brother on the slide. Maybe Jack has a point. If I choose smaller goals to work on, maybe it'll help. "He has a project due a week before spring break. On ancient Egypt. If he passes that, I guess that would feel like a success?"

I'll send him to the Egyptian exhibitions while he waits for me at work.

"Sounds good to me," Jack says.

I peek at him, and he smiles. "You're doing your best. I'm bloody impressed."

His tender words burrow into my chest, and I hide my thankfulness in another sip of coffee.

"I'm gonna make some other changes too."

"What do you have in mind? Less paying Milo to get to bed?"

I groan. "I'll try. But no, I meant I gotta get out of customer-service rep and use my degree. Look for other jobs."

"Sounds like a great plan. I'd be happy to review your resume and application letters if you'd like?"

"I'm totally taking you up on that." He laughs, and I set the cup down between us. "I better . . . talk to him."

Jack stops me with a warm press of his hand against my knee. "Let me?"

For the first time, Jack sounds nervous. Perhaps he thinks

I'll tell him to butt out? But I won't. I have no idea what to say to Milo.

Jack's offer eases the weight off my shoulders. "Would you?"

He squeezes my knee and stands. "It'd be my pleasure, Ben."

I sink back against the bench and watch Jack turn into a silhouette. He mirrors my brother, sitting opposite him atop the slide platform, legs bent, back resting against a wooden beam.

I palm the carvings of lovebirds and breathe deeply. My keys burn in my pocket, and I suppress the urge to fish them out and scratch other initials into the wood.

Chapter Fourteen

JACK

CRAMMED ON A TINY PLATFORM OF SPLINTERED WOOD, MILO and I stare out over the ocean. Gulls swoop toward jagged rocks, and lights twinkle on the distant hills.

Air whistles around us.

I shift. Milo senses me moving and sinks his chin to his chest. His hair hangs forward, almost long enough to curtain his eyes.

"Can I say something?"

He shrugs.

"I'm sorry, Milo."

He glances up, frowning as though he expected me to have a go at him. It wrenches my heart.

I understand Ben's reaction, and I get Milo's too. It's not easy for either of them.

"He tricked me."

Ben is slumped forward on the bench, elbows on his knees, cradling his coffee.

"I think he needed this outing—" Milo interrupts with a burst of frustration and I hold up my hand. "I'm not saying the way he went about it was right. Your brother is aware and sorry for that. But this drive out here? Having an adventure away from the usual chores? He needed that."

He needed it, and damn I needed to give it to him.

Milo's lip wobbles. "How many times do I have to say I don't want to leave our house?" He sniffs. "It's the only thing left of them."

A lump fills my throat.

I get it.

Get how achingly impossible it is to say and do the right thing.

"I can't imagine how badly you are hurting." A breeze washes past us. "Or how badly your brother is."

"He doesn't care."

I tuck a finger under Milo's wet chin and steer his tear-puffed face toward mine. "Ben picks you up every day from school. He takes you bird watching, does your laundry, makes sure you shower and wash your hair."

Milo blinks hard.

I continue, softly, "Does that sound like a man who doesn't care?"

His breath skips toward a sob. "I have five hundred and twenty-seven dollars in my sock drawer. He's anal about shampooing. And a couple of months ago, he bought an insane amount of chicken-pea luncheon meat to get me talking again."

His laugh squeaks, and I chuckle with him. I remember the meat. An insane amount is right.

Milo glances to his brother. "God, he looks tired and miserable, doesn't he?"

"He looks worried." Beautiful, and unreachable.

The soles of Milo's shoes squeal over the wood. "He looks like he needs fish 'n' chips for dinner."

I smile. "I love a good crumbed fish and kumara chips. Especially if they come with a view over the beach."

Milo positions himself to slide. "I'll lead the fantail to the truck."

He sinks down the tunnel slide and strides to Ben on a mission. Their faces glow in the lowering sun, and Ben steals my heart by cocking the mother of all forgiving grins. He pulls Milo into a hug and looks over his shoulder toward me.

When Milo waves me over, I jump off the platform and follow them to the truck.

Ben pauses at the passenger door. "We'll wait in the truck first, Jack. Go to your open house."

I open my door and hop in.

Ben does the same, protesting, "I mean it. You came all this way for inspiration."

Ben startles when he realizes he climbed into the middle. Our sleeves brush and I don't give a damn about the small touches we've traded. This moment is bigger than propriety.

I'll tone it down again tomorrow.

I reach over him and draw the belt over his hips. His lower stomach undulates under my skimming knuckles. I click it into the buckle.

Ben's shallow breath tickles over my jaw.

I pull back and eye Milo and Ben as I start the truck. "The yellow-eyed penguin lives in the forest. True or false?"

Chapter Fifteen

JACK

AT THE END OF THE SCHOOL DAY, WHILE I'M LOOKING OVER Ben's resume and job application letters, Principal Ryan waltzes into my classroom.

At her side is a man in worn jeans and a leather belt that matches his muddy shitkickers. He has a lazy smile, dark eyes, and a cleft chin. I've never seen someone look less like a teacher.

Principal Ryan smiles. "Meet Mort Campbell, Jack Pecker."

Must be the teacher taking over for Mrs. Stacey during her maternity leave. "Welcome to the industrial arts," I say. "We're all about saws, drills, soldering irons, and unclogging the 3D printer nozzle."

Mort laughs, and I catch him measuring me up. It's a glance of a heartbeat—my bet unconscious at that—but my gay-dar pings immediately.

"Mort will start after the spring break."

A gust of wind rushes through the room, and Ben steps inside my classroom. He's wearing jeans with a worn patch at his inner thigh and boots, and he's clasping a navy towel against his chest.

He glides in with a charmed, oblivious smile as though he's walked in a million times before, though this is his first time. "Hey, Jack." His gaze drifts to the principal and Mort Campbell and he halts. "I'm sorry. You're busy."

Principal Ryan's brow shoots up. "Benjamin McCormick."

Ben waves meekly. "Hey, Principal Ryan."

She sizes him up as if calculating his maturity or searching for a suggestion that our relationship is problematic.

I smile over gritted teeth. I hate the way she's looking between us. Hate the questions firing in her head.

I want Ben to leave.

I want him to come again later.

Ben steps back, twisting on his heel, and realization flashes across his face. The realization I don't want him here.

My heart punches up my throat. "Wait, Ben. Please."

He pauses and warily slips to the corner of the room.

"I won't be a moment," I say.

He nods, and busies himself in studying the shelves of student birdhouses.

I rip my attention back to Principal Ryan, who peers from Ben and back to me, her lips pressed in a concerned line. I hold her gaze steady. *There's nothing to hide here.*

Nothing going on at all.

Nothing.

My stomach twists.

Mort says something I miss, and Principal Ryan nods.

The heat of Ben's surreptitious glances fire cannonballs in my gut.

"I look forward to working here." I take Mort's extended

hand. He stares at me as he squeezes one beat too long. Nothing Principal Ryan would notice. But I notice.

Something clatters to the floor in the corner of the room.

Ben notices, too.

"Sorry," Ben mumbles. "Slippery little fucker."

A fond ache in my chest wars with an internal groan.

"Let's continue the tour," Principal Ryan says. She and Mort leave slowly. At the door, she glances at me. "I'm catching up with Howie at the villa this weekend."

It takes all my effort to keep my smile breezy. "Send my regards."

"I always do."

She leaves, but her caution lingers.

Ben has set the towel he brought on a workbench and leans against the shelves with a bounce of his foot. He stuffs his fingers into his pockets, thinks better of it, and pulls them out again with the inside lining. He pokes it back in with an annoyed growl.

I run my fingers over my jaw, prickly from almost a week of not shaving.

"Bad timing, huh?" Ben says.

"It's fine."

I draw closer, but Principal Ryan's last words help maintain a good few feet between us.

"Nice birdhouses," he says. He pulls one off the shelf and admires it. "This one's my brother's."

"There are no name tags. How do you know?"

He chuckles and twists the birdhouse around. Burned into the back: "For Sale. Very cheep."

I rest my ass against the workbench and fold my arms against a heady urge to slide my palm around his nape and kiss out every bird fact and pun in him. It would be beautiful. It might be never-ending.

Ben keeps glancing at the towel.

I lift a questioning brow.

He laughs at himself, sets Milo's birdhouse back on the shelf, and plucks up the towel. With trembling fingers, he extends it to me. "Because, you know . . ."

He watches as I carefully tuck it against my chest. My thumb rubs up and down the edging.

He tries to stuff his hand in his pocket again, but those pants are too damn tight on him. "I thought about wearing the *Say Please and I'll Bend Over* T-shirt as a joke, but I'm glad I didn't."

Christ. "Rather glad myself."

"Principal Ryan looked at me like I was here to suck your cock." He pauses. "The towel probably didn't help."

I choke the towel against my chest. This guy will be the death of me.

He sighs. "I know that can't happen. So, a new teacher, huh?"

My voice is borderline husky, "Mr. Campbell is filling in for a teacher on maternity leave."

"He's hot, hmm?"

Ben's fishing but I don't give in to it. "Your type, is he?"

He scowls at me.

Salty air washes into the classroom along with Luke. "Jack, have you seen the new guy? I think we might have a third member for our club. Oh, hello. Ben, right? We met at the supermarket. I helped you restack tuna cans?"

I have told Luke about Ben, of course. He knows of Ben's fascination with birds and our adventures together. He doesn't know what they mean to me, though.

They eye each other. Ben, with tight eyes and an even tighter smile.

He's killing, killing, killing me.

Milo catches my eye through the window. His backpack is a

ginormous sack at his back. I wave as Ben whips up a hurried 'goodbye.'

"I've got a couple of tweaks on your resume and cover letters. Do you want to take them?"

"Show me later?" He trots toward the door. "I've got a small Milo-related goal to see through."

"His presentation?"

He points me a finger gun, just like that first day. "He will not be emused."

I laugh at the pun and turn back to Luke, who gives me a funny look.

My smile fades.

Chapter Sixteen

BEN

I'M HUNCHED OVER MY OVERHEATED LAPTOP ON MY BED. THE space heater is blasting, and a wall buffers me from Milo's prying eyes.

He's schlepping about in the kitchen, opening and shutting cupboards. Always on the hunt for food, that kid. Nevermind that we ate microwaved lasagna twenty minutes ago.

I review the itinerary I've been making for the approaching long weekend. Milo's teachers have a professional development workshop and since we get Friday free, a trip to the Kapiti Coast is in order. A whole weekend of breathing in the salty spring air and peering at protected birds.

Jack has half of Friday free—a tidbit I've been mulling over for weeks. Would it be weird to invite him? I'd hate for him to be alone the whole weekend.

I should ask.

But he might turn me down . . .

A knock rattles the front door and Milo's feet thump heavily toward it.

"Jack!" Milo says.

Speak of the devil.

Jack's voice leaks through the wall. He's asking how my bucko's doing and what in Christ he's eating. I grin.

"Where's your brother?"

Milo might have answered, but I don't hear him over my ridiculously eager shout. "In here."

Jack raps at my door and pokes his head in. "Ben," he says with a smile I've missed, even though I had the privilege of seeing it this morning.

"Come in and shut the door. Milo's not allowed in here."

Jack enters, and the latch clicks behind him. He stands half a room away, gaze flickering over the desk that's piled with rolls of wrapping paper, the first aid kit I bought after Milo's fall, a box of summer clothes, and extra toilet paper and paper towels.

He's kicked off his boots—likely lined up on the veranda outside—and there's a tiny hole at the big toe.

He scans my outfit: bushman socks—thick woolly tubes that reach mid-calf—shorts, a T-shirt, and a fleece robe. Let's say I wasn't expecting company.

"I've wondered for months what your room looks like."

Weird this is the first time he's seen it, despite how often he sits across from me at the kitchen table, one wall over.

Honestly, I thought he'd have peeked inside when I wasn't here—I wouldn't have cared—yet it's a curiously warm realization that he's respected my space.

He eyes my stylish outfit again and his lips lift on a smile. I surge with the need to ask him along next weekend. I open my mouth and freak out last second. "Thanks for the help on my applications. I made the tweaks you suggested and sent them off."

"You thanked me yesterday."

I know, but nervous idiots like to repeat themselves. I palm my forehead. "Right. Forgot."

"I'm happy to help." He glances to the laptop. "Why exactly isn't Milo allowed in here?"

"It's not porn!"

We turn into statues. Sometimes I really wonder about myself.

Jack clears his throat. "I thought perhaps you were looking at real estate?"

Oh, right.

I shuffle over on the soft bed. "Nope. Have a look."

Jack hesitates, then slings himself next to me. The mattress protests and bounces under me. He stuffs pillows behind him and peers at my screen. "Kapiti Island Bird Sanctuary?"

I tell him my plans for Milo. "It's a surprise."

Jack measures me with a warm, appraising look. "He'll love it."

Do you want to come with us?

He blinks and focuses on the laptop. His body shifts away from mine, minuscule but noticeable.

I bite back the question. I feel it like a cold shiver. He'll say no. He has to. "What brings you to our cottage?"

A puzzled frown follows his tentative question, "Date night?"

It's Friday. Fuck! "Oh right."

He swings his feet off the bed. "I'll let you get dressed."

"Don't leave. I mean"—I cough drily against a fist and hope it sounds real—"I got a cold. Throat is flared up."

He eyes me carefully. "That's no good."

"Yeah, I probably shouldn't spread the germs, so . . ."

"You're staying in?'

"Looks like I'm playing games with you two tonight. What about a round of *Settlers of Catan*?"

∼

AFTER A NIGHT OF BOARD GAMES AND RESTLESS SLEEP, I WAKE Saturday morning to the sound of Milo humming.

I don a fleece robe and stumble into the kitchen. I'm pretty sure I'm seeing things.

Milo's at the table, and there's no Cocoa Puffs in sight.

Instead, the surface is covered with a large placard, felt tip pens, a glue stick, and text printed in a horrible blocky font.

But never mind the ugliness.

"*You're doing your assignment?*"

He mocks me with a heavy dose of sarcasm. "Nah, this is for fun."

He swipes glue over a cut-out text and slaps it down next to the pyramid he's drawn.

I pick up a text block and read it. Sounds good to me. "I'm impressed you started without prompting. All those trips to Te Papa helping, huh?"

"And Wikipedia."

This is good. This is great, right?

Exactly the improvement the school wants to see in Milo.

I frown as he slaps another three texts on the poster, and calls it done. "You're ready to hand it in?"

He picks up a felt and nods. "You're right. I gotta do a better title."

I shake off a tiny thread of concern. This is more than Milo has done for school in forever. "Okay, I'm making a call. When you're finished we'll do some errands. Then we can grab the binoculars and head to the town belt before we go to Te Papa." I say this last part on a yawn.

"You're working today?" he moans.

I feel for him. "Yup, and you're tagging along. Check out another exhibition or something."

I leave him grumbling and hit the creaky patio, dialing. I

get sent straight to voicemail. I rest against a supporting beam, corner digging into my bicep.

"Hey Talia, when are you back from Germany? The time difference is killing me. Have you smoked a joint in a cute bar in Amsterdam yet? Thanks for the postcard from the penis museum in Iceland. Real classy. Also reminds me how little I've had of it the last year. Anyway, update after ignoring your last message. Sorry, this kid stuff is still kicking my ass"— I glance through the open door to Milo—"but maybe we're slowly finding our groove?"

I notice Jack a couple of yards from the veranda, half shrouded by the lemon tree, emptying food into the compost bins.

"How much did you hear?"

He shuts the compost bin and rests a bucket atop the lid. "Amsterdam has amazing cheese. Real tasty stuff."

He heard it all, then. Including the bit about the penises, and not having much of it.

I fight a prickly blush—not something I'm used to in regard to sex. Hell, I've taken and received enough dick pics to start my own penis museum.

Jack eyes me likes he wants to ask a question but presses his lips together. I'd thought our friendship was deepening, but ever since I went to his classroom, he's withdrawn again.

I get it.

But it sucks.

"I'm doing a run to the supermarket." Jack fishes his keys from his pocket, and I'm thrown back to Milo, blood streaming down his face, my fingers stuck in Jack's pocket as he confidently calmed me. "Ben?"

I look up from his pocket. "Sorry, what?"

He might be trying not to smile, but a twinkle in his eye gives him away. "If you're planning on stocking up, there's space in the truck."

A yawn yanks through me. "You don't have to. We were heading to the town belt after a shop."

"I can drop you off wherever you'd like to go."

I fail to school my enthusiasm. "We're coming with you."

"I'm finished!" Milo yells behind me.

I grin proudly toward Jack. "He did his assignment. He actually did it!"

I want Jack's approval more than I care to admit, and he gives it to me. A soft curve of his wide lips.

I clutch my phone, and oops! I never finished my message. The call is still rolling.

I rattle off a goodbye to Talia. "I think you just caught a glimpse of my family life. . . ."

Chapter Seventeen

BEN

I DON'T SLEEP WELL THE NEXT NIGHTS, AND I'M TIRED AND grumpy when I find Milo gone from his room on Thursday morning.

I have a suspicion he snuck to his old room again, and I'm right. I grumble under my breath and grab his school supplies from the cottage. I toss them onto Milo's childhood bed and he wakes with a start. "Get dressed. We're leaving for school in twenty."

He groans and rolls over.

"I mean it. I'm not in the mood for chasing you to school."

I whirl around to find Jack paused in the hallway, eyeing me worriedly. He's wearing his usual canvas pants and tight T-shirt, and he's in the process of slipping on a flannel shirt. He slides the second arm into the sleeve and shoves up the cuff to his elbow. "You okay, Ben?"

I shrug, dragging toward the kitchen and the promise of coffee.

I help myself to a mug, pass one to Jack, and slump against the counter. The cup burns my fingers and I almost drop it.

"What's the matter?" he asks.

"Work sucked yesterday."

"Shitty day?"

"My manager wants me to work the long weekend."

"I thought you have a trip planned?"

"So did I. This coffee is not strong enough. Or sweet enough. Or fizzy enough. This is definitely a Fanta day."

"Fanta-free fridge here." He offers me a sympathetic smile. "Sounds like some rough luck."

"I tried compromising. Said I'd do multiple weekends in a row, but she wouldn't have it. Apparently my request for days off wasn't accepted."

"Sorry this weekend won't be the one you envisioned."

"Ces't la vie, right?" I shrug. "I'm just glad it was a surprise and I don't have to let Milo down."

He cards a hand through his hair. He looks like he wants to close the distance between us and wrap me into a hug. But he refrains. He always does.

He turns and clatters about with pans and bowls. I spy eggs coming out of the fridge.

The amazing smell of scrambled egg fills the air.

Jack works at the stove as I finish my coffee. His back muscles tighten as he jiggles the pan.

He ladles eggs on a plate, butters a piece of toast, and turns to me.

Milo's yawn rips down the hallway, bringing me to the present.

"Thanks for the coffee. I need to get myself ready. Let you eat in peace."

I start to leave, and Jack halts me. He hands me the plate. "Those are for you. Eat up."

"But this is your breakfast."

He steps aside and I see a second and third loaded plate. He hands me a fork. "You look like you need protein."

"Because of the bags under my eyes?"

"And the sallow cheeks."

I grin and follow him to the dining room and slide into a seat at the table. I take a greedy bite before Jack has decided where to sit. "Holy shit. This is delicious." I cram more of the cheesy egg into my mouth. "I think your intentions are backfiring."

He stands at the end of the table, gaze prickling with laughter. "How's that?"

"I wanna keep the sallow cheeks if it means you give me more of your"—I sweep my gaze down and linger at his crotch —"protein."

He hurriedly slides into the adjacent seat, and I'm beyond sure he doesn't mean for our knees to knock.

Jack calls out for Milo to grab his eggs from the kitchen.

Then it's the three of us, playing gaze-tag over our plates.

I have no idea what's happening. But it's turning out to be an unusually warm start to the day.

WARMTH THAT DOESN'T CARRY TO THE AFTERNOON. I LEAVE work and dash into rain. Rain. And more rain.

It angles perfectly, hitting my face and sluicing down my neck and under my jacket.

I need Fanta, pronto.

I race to my car, where an orange puddle greets me on the passenger seat. I'm not sure I'm more upset that it's seeped deeply into the cracked vinyl, or that I've barely a mouthful of the good stuff to drink.

I find a towel in the backseat—along with Milo's jacket.

I chuck the towel over the mess and steer out of the parking lot. I'll postpone the trip to the supermarket and head to Milo. I can collect him from class and give him his jacket.

Yep. It's a plan.

I shiver from the damp. "I have this. I have this."

Jack calls and my car is just fancy enough I can put him on Bluetooth.

I steer into the left lane—no tunnel for me today. I'll head around the bays. Should be almost as fast and have better reception.

"Jack. You done for the day? I'm headed to Kresley now."

Jack's voice tumbles toward me. "Ben. Glad I caught you."

I sit straighter, lighten up on the gas. "What's up?"

"Luke and Sam asked me to ref a soccer game and have dinner after, so . . ."

"You won't be home this evening."

He pauses. "Right. I wanted to let you know."

A fluttery feeling hits my belly. Letting me know. That's . . . thoughtful. He's never done it before, and it's not like he owes me an explanation.

"Have fun at dinner. Not too much fun." I laugh.

"They've invited another teacher, too. New guy at Kresley."

I tense. "Mr. Campbell?"

"Right."

I grip the wheel. "Is this a set up?"

He pauses. "It might be."

"Yeah. Cool. Cool. Have fun."

"It's just dinner."

"So have fun eating. The food, not . . ." I cringe. This is

why Jack would never give me a shot. I'm *totally* rocking the maturity thing.

My spirits take a dive.

"Did you know albatross have the lowest divorce rate?"

"Albatross, what?" Jack sounds amused—and not particularly surprised at my random outburst.

"In the bird world. They are ridiculously faithful to one another."

"Admirable trait."

"They always come back to their partner."

"Ben?"

"Sadly, so many are attracted to tuna long lines, and . . . well, their partners live on always waiting, wondering, hoping—"

Jack is quiet, and I pretty much want to disappear into my seat.

I jumpstart the next sentence with a laugh. "More on the albatross tomorrow. After my date night."

I enunciate the last part and it's left hanging between us. "Ben—"

"Have a great night. I'm about to hit the tunnel. Gotta go. Bye!"

I PARK OUTSIDE THE SCHOOL. THE FRONT THIS TIME.

It's a shorter distance to Wing C and my bro.

My phone dings with an email notification.

Thank you for your application for the position of Communications Advisor for the Department of Conservation. I regret to inform you that you have not been selected for an interview.

Right. Got it.

I close my eyes and lean back.

"I still have this," I remind myself. "I have this."

I grab Milo's jacket, pull the hood down on mine, and splash to Wing C. The bell rings and children start tripping out of classrooms.

I wend my way toward Milo's class.

I catch him stuffing his bag, close to Mrs. Devon's desk.

The classroom is neat as a pin.

Mrs. Devon spots me, nods cordially, and beckons me to her.

My phone bursts to life, and on automatic I check. Talia.

God her timing sucks. It must be the middle of the night there.

Probably a drunk call, which are always the funniest, and I could do with some funny.

Mrs. Devon gives me a reproachful look so I ignore the call and stuff my phone into my ass pocket.

I wield my most charming grin. Milo mumbles about waiting in the car.

I give him his jacket and the keys. "Fanta exploded on the front seat. Sit on the towel."

He trundles off and I meet Mrs. Devon's eyes. She's never been one to smile, and I don't expect it. But I have a hopeful jump in my belly that she is seeing improvement with Milo.

"I'm glad you popped in, Benjamin."

I joke. "It's hard to tell, what without the usual cue of a smile."

She grimaces. Not quite a smile, but it'll do. "I finished grading assignments."

She rummages through a pile of posters and pulls out Milo's. "We'll be having another term assignment after the spring break. It's a three-week one, requiring each child to write an essay on an influential world figure. I hope he exerts himself more than he has this term."

I glance over the poster I'm pinching. A typed remark is stapled to the side.

Two out of eighteen points.

"The two points are for the artwork."

"Right." My voice is dry. "I thought the information on the Egyptians was decent."

"It is. It is also directly cut and pasted from Wikipedia."

"He researched online. I thought he rewrote the main points . . ."

"Perhaps you should spend more time with Milo on his assignments and less time schmoozing with his teachers."

My stomach balls into a knot.

I don't like what Mrs. Devon's insinuating, but I'm bereft of fucking words.

"Right," I squeeze out again. "I'll work more closely with him."

"You do that. Excuse me, I have another meeting."

I back to the exit, rolling the poster tightly.

"Right."

I hoof it out of Wing C and into the downpour.

Milo doesn't look at me when I slip into the driver's seat, and I don't particularly want to look at him right now, either.

My chest deflates and I start the car saying the only thing I can think of. "Shortcuts never end well."

Chapter Eighteen

JACK

I STARTLE AT MRS. DEVON SHUFFLING THROUGH MY CLASSROOM door as I'm packing up. "Do you have a moment?"

Not the kind of question that allows for anything less than an 'of course.'

"Come in. Take a seat." She doesn't take the offered chair. She pushes her glasses up her nose and nods tightly. "This won't take long."

"Is this about Milo's loose tongue? Because I feel his maturity is slowly improving—"

"This has to do with Milo and his brother."

I stiffen, perch on a nearby stool, and meet her eye. "What's your concern?"

"Milo's called you Jack a few times in class. He has plenty of stories about how close you are with him and his brother."

"It's no secret I'm working on their house. Our paths cross."

"You're not getting too close, are you?" she asks shrewdly.

"The particulars of our relationship do not concern you."

Her gaze pinches with worry. "Be careful, Jack."

I keep my voice firm and even. "I'll remind you that there is nothing in my contract that prohibits me from having relationships with parents outside of school."

Strictly speaking.

"Said like a man who looked it up. Regardless, school policy discourages employees from dating their student's caregivers."

"No one said anything about dating. Besides that fact, I'm part-time staff and Milo is not in my class full time."

"You are held to a higher standard of behavior than in other professions. Your colleagues and other parents will judge everything you do on and off school grounds."

"Patricia—"

"If that's not enough, their situation is fragile. Benjamin and Milo are emotionally vulnerable. Nothing to take advantage of."

The accusation slams into my chest. I walk to the door and open it for her, barely suppressing my anger. "Thank you for coming, Mrs. Devon."

She walks past me, pauses, and shakes her head. "He's just a kid in oversized clothes."

I wait until she's out of earshot, then slam the door behind her.

∽

I'M ANGRY.

Angry more at myself than Mrs. Devon.

Angry, because she has a point. Angry because while I haven't crossed a line, I spend every day flirting with it.

I can't let this situation with Ben progress any further than friendship. My relationships with colleagues, the job I love, and my dream villa depend on it.

I arrive at Luke and Sam's and promise myself to focus on the moment. Maybe there will be sparks between Mort and me if I open myself to it.

We dine on shepherd's pie and enjoy a rich pinot noir in the great room. The hearty scent of onion, garlic, and baked cheese scents the air. The food tastes delicious. But the mashed potato and minced meat are not as comforting as they're supposed to be.

"You worked on the house?" Mort asks. His voice has a husky quality to it as if he navigates through life laughing.

We chat about the remodeling, and Sam and Luke's gazes ping-pong between us.

Interest glimmers in Mort's eyes.

"What brings you to Wellington?" I ask.

He hesitates. "My dad passed away."

"Sorry to hear that, mate."

"Wish I could say the same." He doesn't elaborate, and we don't force the issue.

"How do you like the teachers at Kresley?" Sam asks in the sudden stretched silence.

I mutter, "How do you like Mrs. Devon?"

Three frowns land on me, and I curse my unprofessional outburst.

I prod at the half-eaten meat on my plate while Sam and Luke take over talking.

Ten minutes into it, someone kicks my leg under the table. Luke is smiling at me. "Jack. Mind helping me with dessert?"

In the corner of the kitchen, Luke fixes whipped cream on a Pavlova. Sam and Mort are engaged in conversation ranking their favorite arcades.

Luke whispers, "What's going on, mate?"

"Nothing." I slice kiwifruit and decorate the top of the dessert. "What do you think of Ben?"

Luke pauses. "How do you mean?"

"Just . . . in general."

"I only met him for two minutes. What do you want me to think of him?"

I rub my beard, fingers sticky from kiwifruit juice. I'm going to smell of fruit until I shower. "Never mind. Mort seems like a nice guy."

"Jack . . ."

"Let's serve this dessert."

At the table, I serve Mort a wide grin. "You teach science. Tell me, did you know the albatross have the lowest divorce rate?"

∿

I ARRIVE HOME AROUND MIDNIGHT AND COLLAPSE INTO BED. What a miserable attempt at throwing my romantic attentions elsewhere.

Forcing myself to engage with Mort had felt rote and strained.

I scrub my face through a groan.

If I'd only left a minute earlier from class today. If only Mrs. Devon hadn't offered me her unwelcome opinion.

I'd still be jockeying to stay on this side of the line.

I close my eyes on her words echoing in my head.

I need to maintain distance. I need to tell Ben to stop flirting with me.

Wood suddenly groans and creaks. Someone is in the house. Milo sneaking into his bedroom, probably.

I wait for the sounds to stop before slowly planting my bare feet on the cold floor. I'll double check Milo hasn't sleep-walked into the bathroom like he once did, then message Ben.

The oriental rug prickles against my soles as I steal into the hallway. A sniff coming from the master bedroom has me swiftly moving toward it. That was not the sound of Milo.

I pause at the half-opened door. In a heartbeat, I shove aside my resolutions to set better boundaries.

Ben is kneeling on the hardwood floor between the two sets of windows. Moonlight boldly stamps elongated squares on the floor. He's wearing a night T-shirt, boxers, and jandals.

He sees me and glances to his feet, wet with dew from tromping over the garden.

"Jack," he says and thinly laughs. "I was just . . . taking a tour down memory lane."

I approach slowly. He's laughing but his eyes are devoid of humor.

"I, uh, didn't mean to wake you."

"I wasn't asleep." Even if I was, I wouldn't care.

"Phew." His gaze shoots from my bare feet to my boxers and thin T-shirt. He averts his eyes the moment ours connect. "You don't have to, like, stay up for me if you're tired."

I crouch before him, one knee on the cool floor. "Are you alright?"

"Because of my bags and sallow cheeks?"

"Because you look like you're drowning."

"Well, guess I can't look my awesomest self all the time."

"Not bad," I quickly correct, "just lost."

"Lost. Nope. Totally know where I'm supposed to go, but I"—his voice breaks and it echoes in my chest—"I don't know how to get there. At all."

"Oh, Ben. What's going on?"

Ben rests his head against the floral wallpaper. His Adam's apple juts hard as he swallows.

"It's a horrible thing to think, 'what would my life be like if Mum and Dad hadn't decided on a weekend trip to the Waiarapa that day?' It's a stupid question, and the answer won't change anything. And, I'm happy with Milo and being here for him. I love him. I do."

I clasp his warm knees. "I know you do."

His lip wobbles. He tries to laugh off the rising emotion. Tries to clear his voice.

It pinches. "But sometimes I daydream about it, you know? What it would be like if it was just me. What it would be like if I had someone to help raise him. Discipline him. Take him on adventures so I could have more downtime. Read a book. Catch up on sleep."

"Did something particular happen today?"

He bows his head onto his knees.

I wrap an arm around his back. His silent sobs jerk my arm. I rub his warm neck, and steer him to my chest. He grabs my waist, fingers digging at my ribs. His breath pulses through my thin shirt.

I breathe him in and tighten my hold. "Ben?"

"He got a two out of eighteen. I supervised that assignment and thought it was okay. Mrs. Devon caught me picking him up from class, and—"

Ben's pain lances through me with every guttural sob, and I clutch him tighter, rub circles over his shuddering back.

"—She didn't even have to say much, you know. She handed me his assignment, and it was all in the look she gave me. How much I'm messing up. Because I am. I'm messing up. And not just with Milo. I got three job rejections—I wasn't even asked for an interview, and I forgot my pin code to my card because I don't sleep. I barely ever sleep. I lie in bed, telling myself to. But all I can think about are all the things that need doing, and all the things I want to be doing instead."

It rips through me, the words, the crumbling of his voice. I push back his hair. Tuck his bangs behind his ear only to have it fall over his face again. "If you need me to help more—"

"It's not your problem. It's *so* not your problem. But I see you, and I want it to be." He sniffs and tries to pull away, but I keep him close. "I'm sorry. I'm meant to be funny. Meant to crack jokes and laugh, not . . ."

"You're allowed to cry."

"Will you stay in our lives?" His moist breath sieves through to my stomach. "Will you stay in our lives and be our friend, please? Will you stay in our lives and be our friend even if I'm such a flirt?"

This guy is breaking my heart. Fuck it. "Flirt all you like. I've got you."

Chapter Nineteen

BEN

I CRACK EGGS INTO A GLASS BOWL. CUT FETA INTO LARGE squares on a china plate.

All the utensils I need are right here. Now to just . . . throw them together.

I duck into the bottom cupboard for a pan, but the main house has far too many choices. Non-stick bottom? Cast iron?

I choose the latter and emerge to find Jack standing barefoot in the kitchen doorway. His navy boxers outline a generous package, and the night T-shirt I'd sobbed against is clasped against his chest.

His eyes dart around, taking in my freshly showered hair, long-sleeved T-shirt, and black jeans.

My jandals slap against the tile as I walk toward him.

"Jack, morning."

He searches my face for a sign I remember last night.

I more than remember my crazy outburst. Not my finest moment.

"Morning," he says carefully.

The pan is weighing my hand and I set it on the counter.

"I was hoping you'd stay out of the kitchen a little longer. Give me time to surprise you with breakfast."

He spots the food on the bench and eyes me warily. "Do you know how to scramble eggs?"

"They're eggs. They get messed with a fork. How hard can it be?"

"I've seen you shop. Your cart is all add water or microwave on high for seven minutes."

"Must I remind you where your assumptions led you with the binoculars?"

Jack's lips twitch. "They led me right here."

"That's right."

I move back to the stove, and Jack grabs a drink of water before making coffee.

He sets a coffee in front of me and peers over the rim of his mug, carefully assessing.

I hope my blotchy, puffed face from last night has returned to its former gently-freckled glory.

After a sip, he asks, "How are you holding up?"

"With the eggs?"

He shoots me a no-nonsense look. "With Milo. With sleep. All of it. You left so suddenly."

I had to. The intimacy became more than I could cope with. I wanted to stay. I wanted to ask if he would curl up with me in my bed all night. But I didn't want to put Jack in the position where he had to turn me down.

Didn't want to hear him turning me down.

I pulled away, thanked him, and left.

"Look, I'm sorry about my performance last night."

"Don't be."

I rub my nape. "Right. Well too bad, because I'm as sorry as sorry can be. Embarrassed as embarrassed can be, too. Maybe even mortified as—"

Jack's lips press together. "Cut it, Ben. Are you okay?"

I grab the salt grinder. I see him patiently waiting, and whisper. "Yeah. Thank you for being there."

The small, pathetic words aren't enough to convey my gratitude. But they are the only words I find.

Jack sidles closer and gently nudges my elbow with his.

He flashes me a smirk. "How much salt do you think those eggs need?"

I stop grinding and laugh. "Can I maybe watch you make them instead?"

He bumps his hip against mine and takes over the food.

"Is Milo up?" he asks.

"Watching *Avatar* with a bowl of Cocoa Puffs. We have half an hour before he screams bloody murder for a Fanta."

Jack shakes his head. "The junk food has to go."

I snort. "Good luck trying to convince either of us. But please go ahead and do your worst."

Jack pours the eggs into a hot pan and puts on his teacher voice. "I can be quite persuasive."

It has an immediate—rather fizzy—effect on me. The urge to flirt is like a dry throat tickle demanding to be coughed.

I barely hold back. "What are your plans this beautifully gray Friday?"

"After today's workshop, I'm checking out wallpaper and moldings, then shopping for real food." He gives me a pointed look.

"Hey, I've put broccoli and green stuff in my cart every week for months now."

"And let it rot in your fridge. Nothing but lip service, Ben."

He's right. The term lip service is spiraling my thoughts toward the gutter. "What else you got planned?"

I take the eggs he offers and melt into a moan. Jack jerks his head to me, gripping his own plate.

"Seriously," I say over another mouthful. "You could ask me anything and I'd say yes as long as you always feed me."

He recomposes. "Eggs are nothing. I'm cooking for us all tonight. You, me, and Milo."

"For another question you want me to say yes to?" I run a flirtatious tongue over my bottom lip.

He rolls his eyes. "For your health."

Chapter Twenty

JACK

BEN HAS BEEN EYEING ME ALL EVENING. THE DARTING GLANCES fry me with electricity. And like clockwork, Mrs. Devon's voice chimes in my head.

Last night has made my predicament a little tougher to manage, but I will. I might not be able to cross lines, but I sure as hell can be Ben's friend. Let him flirt. I won't fold. I'll be fine.

My finger pulses where I burned it taking out the roasted chicken and vegetables. But it's nothing to the pulsing beat of Ben's gaze.

Ben pivots his attention to Milo. I want to holler. I want to howl.

Milo finishes a third helping of sweet potato and gravy, then looks under the lip of the table where he's been badly hiding his phone. He lifts his head and grins at Ben. His scar turns from pale to dark pink. "I need to call Devansh."

Ben shrugs.

Milo is halfway to the door in the blink of an eye. The boy can move fast when properly motivated.

"Hold it," I say, and he stalls.

I gesture to his plate. "You think that plate magically cleans itself off the table?"

Milo's expression sinks into despair. "Aw, do I have to?"

Ben takes a breath as if preparing for battle, and I'm struck with his sincere wish for someone to help discipline the kid.

I reply before Ben has to. "Yeah, kid. It's the least you can do after someone makes dinner for you."

"Yeah, but . . . I was supposed to call Devansh ten minutes ago."

I nudge the plate toward him. "Better move quickly then."

Milo glares at me and looks to Ben for a save.

Ben mouths "thanks" and sinks into his chair. "You heard the man, bucko."

Milo stomps to the table and makes a loud clatter as he drops his plate and cutlery into the kitchen sink.

The backdoor slams, and Ben cringes.

"Sorry, Jack."

I wave it off. "You finished?"

"It was delicious." He waggles his brow. "You can ask me anything now."

I laugh. "Let me clear up."

Ben jumps to his feet and gathers dishes. "Sit. You cooked, I'll clean." His startlingly dark eyes catch mine and hold for an amused beat. "I'm not quite as stupid as my bro."

"Quite as smart-mouthed, though."

His smile widens. "Appears we are having a fine influence on each other, hmm?"

I grin, my veins skipping with warmth.

My phone rings.

"Hey, Luke."

Ben slows down gathering dishes to listen.

Luke asks me about a game of soccer.

"Soccer game, Sunday? Count me in. Hang on, do you need make numbers?" Ben is violently shaking his head. I grin. "Can I bring another body?"

As soon as I finish the call, Ben shakes his head. "You'll be bringing a body all right. Limp and useless."

"It's a friendly game with Luke and Sam and his son's mates. And I was thinking of leaving you here and taking Milo."

"Oh." He frowns at his plate despite his outburst about not being good at soccer.

I collect my plate, round the table, and pick up the pile he's stacked. I catch a whiff of Ben—spring and wet grass with a dash of musk. "You are more than welcome to come too. I just thought, maybe this way you could have some downtime. To read a book. Catch up on sleep."

He blinks and smiles tenderly.

We shuttle the dishes into the kitchen and split the chore. We both look at the digital clock atop the fridge, and I wait for him to mention date night.

He doesn't.

Maybe he forgot it's Friday.

I don't remind him.

What next hangs in the air as we migrate to the living room. Ben slows his step and scours the room for a reason to stay.

I want to tell him he doesn't need a reason.

He moves towards the open bureau and fingers my home designs.

"What's this?"

"I haven't shown you?" My stomach lurches giddily. I clear my kauri coffee table and unroll the designs.

Ben pins down the curling corners with coasters. "A colored sketch of a house and interiors?"

Not just a sketch. "My dream."

Ben cocks a brow. "Your dream, eh?" He studies the paper. "Detailed."

"I've only been imagining it for eight years."

"Looks like a pretty house."

"House. You're killing me." I sweep a finger toward the exterior. The veranda, cast iron fretwork, metal roof, and timber body. "Not just a house. A turn of the twentieth century villa."

I explode into a gust of enthusiasm as I point out the remodels I'll make to the back of the house, while keeping the character of the front façade. "It's more than a villa. It's my future."

"These drawings are too specific not to be based on a model."

And there's the catch. "Yeah. It's a villa up in Karori."

"The owners not looking to sell?"

"It's owned by a dastardly funny chap with declining health. He's been thinking of moving in with his daughter in Christchurch. He often talks of selling soon. Hell, he knows I have my eye on it—and I'll pay over asking price. But he hasn't settled on a moving date yet."

"It could happen any time?"

"Summer, likely."

"End of this year?"

I groan. "I hope so. I've waited eight already." Albeit, I've only had the entire funds to buy it outright in the last six months. "I'm feeling lucky, though."

I'm relieved to see my passion amuses him. "This is the love of my life. This is my home."

He reads the notes I have about paint. "Down to the carmine and alabaster trimming on the windows?"

"Down to the carmine and alabaster trimming on the windows."

In the distance, Milo calls Ben's name. I stand, and Ben mirrors me.

Static fills the short space between us and I force myself not to step into it.

Milo calls again, and Ben shakes his head with a crooked smile. "Never gives up, that kid."

His hand tentatively shoots to my shoulder and the warmth of his fingers simmers through my shirt. The effect is immediate and tempting, and I steel myself against the impulse to steady the slight tremble running through his arm and pull him tight against me.

He—not entirely cluelessly—meets my eye. "I hope you get what you're looking for, Jack."

He moves away, leaving behind a disquieting flurry in my stomach.

I stare from my home plans to the backdoor he left through. "Me too."

Chapter Twenty-One

JACK

THE LAST WEEK OF CLASSES BEFORE THE SPRING BREAK RACE BY and it's Friday again. It feels like my life is made of Fridays. The whole week feels like one big escalation.

Fridays have my stomach in knots.

Ben was "sick" a couple weeks ago.

He forgot last Friday.

What will happen tonight?

I should encourage him to go out. The two encounters I've had with Mrs. Devon today are enough motivation. Ben had it right. She can say everything in a single look.

Dark clouds spill open when I'm halfway across the netball courts. I raise an arm over my head and jog. Through the silvery sheets of rain, I spot Ben hustling Milo into his car.

He has a vibrant grace about him. Even in miserable weather. No matter how heavy the world is on his shoulders, he summons enough strength to plow forward.

Ben opens his front door and scours over the roof. Is he searching for me?

He's surprised to see me, likely because it's a half day for the kids and he expects the teachers work longer. I've been on break since yesterday but needed to wrap a few things up today.

He pushes the hair out of his eyes. The rain plasters his locks over his ears.

I dash toward him. "You'll get soaked. Get in the car."

"You got plans?"

"Not until later." Hanging out with Milo.

"Then follow us!" He dives into the driver's seat and shuts the door.

He waits for me to flash my lights at him before he sets off.

Before I know it, we're rushing through the rain to the cinema.

We watch a teen film about an underdog sports team and a budding first romance.

Milo sits between us, and I spend the hour and a half not glancing at Ben despite the glances he slides across me every other minute.

I have to convince him to go out tonight.

When the movie's over, we head back home.

I splash after Milo and Ben to the guest cottage. It's close to eight—time for Ben to do his Friday thing.

We drip inside his kitchen and Milo darts to his bedroom bowed over his phone.

Ben collapses onto a chair at the table. I hang up our jackets outside, and return to Ben kicking out his legs and stretching.

I steer my gaze elsewhere—and fast. "I'm ready for a round of Scrabble."

"Really?"

"Milo and I will duke out who can use the Q first."

"Right. Date night." A quirk of disappointment hits his lips. He taps against his mouth with a pathetic cough that I haven't heard for two weeks. "Still not 100 percent."

I should insist he go out. "Let me get you some water for that."

What am I doing?

"Can you color it orange, add some fizz and a fuck-ton of sugar?"

I send him a scathing look. "I'm seriously considering taking over your diet. Feeding you every meal."

He looks at me like he'd let me. I swallow. "Hey, Milo!" I call quickly. "Ready for a game of Scrabble?"

Milo calls from his bedroom. "Slang allowed?"

Ben snorts. "I'm not playing if it's not."

I shake my head. "As long as it's in the dictionary."

"The Urban Dictionary?" Ben is totally unfazed by my no-bullshit narrowed eyes. Just like his brother.

Milo trundles into kitchen. He's changed into a pair of fluffy blue-and-white striped socks. He thumps the board game against my chest in time with his grin. "You set up the board, Mr. Woodpecker. I'm grabbing a Fanta."

I shake my head in exasperation. "I give up on you two."

Insincere words, if ever I have said them.

Ben snags Milo's wrist. His gaze flickers to me and lands on his brother. "Naughty words or sugary poison. Take your pick."

Milo plunks his ass down and huffs at his brother. "What do you choose?"

Ben grimaces. "Yeah, I dunno."

Milo taps his chin, deliberating. "You're choosing the drink, aren't you?"

Ben points a finger gun at him. "Five points to Hufflepuff."

"Slytherin."

"You don't know the capital of Australia. You're not smart enough for Slytherin."

"But cute enough for Hufflepuff?"

"You make a good point. You have no house. I suppose we should commiserate with a drink . . ."

I round behind Ben and settle my hands firmly on his shoulders. His T-shirt is soft and thin, and his muscles jump under my touch. I squeeze once, and a moan rumbles out of him.

I want to rub his shoulders properly.

I peel my hands off him. "Stay seated. You two set up, I'll provide the beverages."

Ben stage whispers to Milo for my overhearing benefit. "Bossy, isn't he?"

Milo giggles. "He treats you like his pet, bro; you should hear him at school."

Rain drums a fierce beat over the cottage.

Spring rain, hot drinks, my two favorite boys hunched over a board game—my night's perfect. I could get used to this.

Water overflows the kettle I'm filling. I snap off the faucet. Christ. What am I doing?

These daydreams are coming too often, lingering too long.

Their situation is fragile. Benjamin and Milo are emotionally vulnerable. Nothing to take advantage of.

Mrs. Devon's words immediately extinguish the dream.

Heavily, I set the kettle on.

I'll call Mort back after the spring break. Focus these increasing romantic urges on someone else. Someone charming enough, older. Emotionally available.

"What the hell?" Ben frowns hard at the Scrabble board. "Did you just projectile spit, bucko?"

Milo scoffs. "I'm not a camel."

I busy myself in pulling mugs out the cupboard.

"Uh-oh. Jack, please tell me that jug has been boiling a really long time."

"Nope." I shut the cupboard.

Ben looks tired and defeated. His Adam's apple juts on a swallow. "I feared as much."

He cocks his head upward and I follow his gaze. Water is collecting in a large yellow circle on the ceiling. Not vapor from a kettle boiling too long. The drywall is saturated.

"Oh, Christ." I switch off the kettle and unplug it.

Sudden leakage can potentially become an emergency.

The drywall might crumble in.

"Milo," I say quickly and firmly, "head to the main house. Ben, grab the necessities and follow. I'll turn the power off and make an emergency repair."

Hopefully I have roofing tar somewhere.

I throw Milo my keys, and his eyes glisten at the prospect of sleeping in the main house. He practically jumps into his rain boots and skips out the door.

He doesn't shut it though, and it rattles against the jamb with the wind.

Ben rubs his biceps warily. "How long will it take to fix?"

I clasp my hands over his, where they dig into his muscle. Our fingers slide together and his eyes shoot to mine.

"Will you manage a night in the main house?"

He looks at me with trust that cascades through me. "Can I sleep with you?"

I hesitate, and he reads it.

"As a friend," he adds, quickly.

A drop of water falls between us, and I usher him into his room, grab a duffel bag and unzip it.

"I've got to stop the dripping, check the attic. Probably need to clear the insulation and put a protective layer across the joists. If I don't have enough roofing tar, I'll work with some tarpaulin sheeting. I have some in the conservatory."

"Jack?"

I stop rambling about repairs and run a hand over my short beard. "Yeah, Ben. You can sleep with me. I'll take care of you."

Chapter Twenty-Two

BEN

I PEER THROUGH MY BINOCULARS, BUT THE RAIN MAKES IT impossible to glimpse into the cottage. Jack is darting back and forth between the houses and has been working close to an hour now.

I shiver against a frigid breeze and drop the binoculars to my chest. I lean against the open back door—a good couple of feet from the downpour that flattens the weeds outside.

Jack finally emerges and clomps across the deck. He stops before me and removes his boots. "I thought you'd go inside."

I lean against the doorframe. "I did. To check on Milo. He's decided playing on his phone in bed is better than hanging out with me. Apparently my agitation agitates him."

"You seem more at ease inside."

"When you're in there," I blurt. "I mean, I just wanted to stand outside in the rain under a full moon and peep at you."

Jack arches a brow. "Ben, you can be honest with me."

"In that case, shove me against this wall and suck—"

"Not that honest."

I push off the doorframe and teeter on the threshold. "I'm kinda nervous. My bedroom is the only one I haven't been back in."

"Let's go in together."

"And undress you."

"Ben . . ." A warning hums in his voice.

I slink backwards inside the house, eyes never leaving Jack. "You're wet. You need dry clothes or you'll catch a cold."

Something soft dances in Jack's tone. "The likes you have? Or a real one?"

Busted.

I toss him a sheepish grin.

He strides inside the house with confidence. I hesitate, and then follow him.

We pass Milo's bedroom first, and I duck my head in to say goodnight. He's half-asleep, and I turn off the lights and shut his door.

The next room is my old bedroom. Jack pauses outside it. "You don't need to go in right away."

I hug my arms. "Yeah, I do. I need to get this over and done with."

My pulse skitters, and I shuffle closer to him. I step inside with his wet sleeve seeping into mine. The hair on his forearm combs against mine and we part again.

The light flickers on and glows over the room.

I panic, but not from the memories gently lapping at the edges of my mind.

Jack has been sleeping in this room.

It's a clean room, but it's not very mature. Too many bright framed pictures of native birds, hand illustrated like something out of a picture book. The wooden carvings of kiwis, tui, and pukekos that I tried to make myself are so amateur it's painful.

Has staying here affected his impression of me?

Worry shades Jack's eyes. "Is it too much, being in here?"

Yes, but not for the reasons it should.

I can't admit that. Too shameful.

The urge to make the room more sophisticated overwhelms me. Floorboards creak as I cross to the window bench. "I wrote an entire paper titled 'The Ecological Footprint of Tourism in New Zealand' sitting here."

There's a soft glimmer of understanding in his eyes.

Heat washes up my throat.

"Did you visit often during your time at university?"

His acknowledgment of my time at university—of my adult age—makes me groan. "Oh fuck, I wear my thoughts on my sleeve."

"Or behind jokes."

I slump onto the window bench, and the cold bites through my jeans. "I'm a terrible person. I came in here expecting to be hit with memories of them, details of them, and instead I'm freaking out about what you think of me."

"Don't freak out, Ben. I think a lot of you."

Jack's smile wanes as he catches me glancing at his mouth. His eyes grow sharper and his posture tenses as though he worries I'll leap on him.

I want to. God, I do.

But only when he wants me to.

Hanging from the ceiling is a wooden seagull painted gray and white. The light glitters over the streaks of childish brushstrokes. The wings and body are strung together with a yellow cord. One pull of the beaded end makes the wings flap.

It should be covered in dust, but the wings are spotless.

Jack tugs the small cord. The wood grates gently as the wings flap up and down, the beak of the gull pushing forward.

"His name's Johnathan."

Jack's eyebrows rise in inquiry. "Johnathan Livingston?"

I fire him a finger gun. "Five points to Gryffindor."

His laugh is full-bodied and deep, and it expands his chest, shifting the damp material. His nipples harden through the T-shirt and goosebumps creep up his arms. I swallow. "You should get out of those clothes."

Jack tugs the T-shirt over his head but the wet material stops budging. Too soaked.

He grunts, and I snort trying to swallow a laugh.

Air shifts as I step forward. Jack senses me moving.

"I'm not trying . . . It's just you're . . ."

"Yeah, I'm stuck," Jack answers for me, voice muffled through the material.

He peeks at me awkwardly from the neck of his shirt like a turtle. I reach forward, fingers tingling at the warmth of his skin before I touch him. I pinch the hem of the shirt and peel it up.

My knuckles skate over goosebumps and damp hair. Jack smells of wood logged with rain and a hint of deodorant. I take one extra breath of it before giving the shirt one last tug.

It pops off and thunks against his wet jeans and my dry ones.

Jack's expression glitters with humor.

Fresh T-shirts must be in a drawer nearby, yet he hesitates.

The hairs on his chest are damp, clinging darkly against his firm muscle. The skin around his nipples pebbles. He's cold, yet his closeness radiates warmly into me.

His green eyes are a match for the color of the feature wall behind him, and for the pillowcases at the head of my bed. So green. And the pupils are dilating.

I breathe in sharply and we both lurch back at the same time.

Jack twists to a chest of drawers and pulls out a nightshirt similar to the one from the night of my crazy outburst.

It is the one.

"I haven't seen a spare mattress," he says.

"That's because I don't have one." Certainly nothing I want to drag in here through the rain, anyway. "If you throw me a pillow, I can make do with the floor."

"No, we can share tonight."

"You sure?" Say yes, please.

"Yes." He unzips his pants.

I whirl around toward the window. The darkness outside and the light inside create a mirroring effect. Arousal builds in my groin.

"Did you want to watch something?"

"I'm kinda tired. How about we . . ."

"Get to bed?"

"Yeah, and chat." I pop open my button and try not to gawk at Jack's reflection as he strips out of his pants. "How bad is the cottage roof?"

I slide my thumbs into the waist of my jeans and stomp out of them.

Jack's turned around and I catch him glance at my ass in the reflection. His voice has a huskiness that reaches to my cock. "We'll have to replace it."

It takes me a moment to process what he's said. Replace it? I freeze. "How long will that take?"

His gaze meets mine in the windowpane. "I'm sorry that it's hard for you being in the main house."

"No. I mean, yes. I mean, it's been getting easier." I face him. We're both in T-shirts and boxers, and my dick is not exactly playing innocent.

Jack notices and shifts around the bed. I make a quick adjustment and approach the other side.

"It'll, ah, take me a couple of days to replace it," he says. "But I can only start once the weather's cleared up."

The forecast predicted rain the next ten days.

I draw back the covers. "You mean that we'll be living with

you for two weeks?"

Jack crosses to the light switch and the room darkens. Too much moonlight fills the room and neither of us escapes seeing one another. "I could ask if Luke and Sam wouldn't mind you staying with them, if you'd prefer?"

"No," I say, a little too quickly.

"Then I'll see about borrowing a roll-out mattress."

I slide under the crisp covers. "Cold, cold, cold."

Jack hops in on his side, and a cool draft of air flows over my chest. I curl onto my side and bunch my body toward his. I stop before touching him, just close enough that a frisson of warmth tingles over my arms and legs.

A dash of desire brightens his gaze, but mostly his eyes hold a warning.

"We're about to have an uncomfortably direct conversation, aren't we?" I ask.

"All part of the adult gig."

I shuffle back an inch. "Lay it on me."

"We need to keep this platonic."

I want to debate him, but I'm sure it'll be fruitless. I'm not sure what metal Jack is made of, but it's strong stuff. No matter how much he likes what he sees, how available I am, he won't give in to me.

I admire and loathe him for it. "Yeah, Jack. We can. I fancy fucking you, but I fancy your friendship more."

I roll onto my back and stare at the glow-in-the dark morepork above my bed that faintly glows through the shadows.

"It's a frustrating situation," Jack says.

I laugh. "You can say that again." I turn my head toward him. He's on his side, one hand stuffed under the pillow, the other splayed in the foot space between us. "But I get it, there's a lot for you to lose. Let's keep it safe. Let's talk."

"What do you want to talk about?"

"You, Jack."

Chapter Twenty-Three

JACK

THERE'S A GOOD FOOT BETWEEN US, AND I'LL DO EVERYTHING to maintain it. To make sure we don't so much as bump toes.

I've never been so annoyed at a ten-day rain forecast.

Never been so thrilled by it.

I wish it darker. Wish I'd closed the curtains. Wish Ben's form would simply be a blanketed lump beside me.

Instead, his pale features glow in the moonlight. The sharp edge of his nose, the dark line of his lips, a bang over his eye that invites me to tuck it back.

A hum of energy thrums between us. The temptation to roll into it is dizzying.

Societal pressures keep me from doing so. Moral doubts. And something else, too. Something I can't quite articulate, but it's there; an invisible rope that resists the pull.

Ben tucks his hands behind his head and the lock over his eye shifts. "What was your childhood bedroom like?"

I pad more blankets between us and twist onto my back. "My room?"

Ben's lips curve up at the edge. "I bet you made your own desk when you were only ten. Probably had a poorly made birdhouse perched in the corner from when you were three and the hammer was too heavy."

I chuckle despite the rawness of the memories suddenly swamping me. "Anything else?"

"I bet it smelled of sawdust and the walls were plastered with hot soccer players." Ben hums. "And you had a shelf— maybe something you made with your dad—that bowed under the weight of CDs and DVDs."

"Some VHS tapes, too," I add. "And the birdhouse I made at 8. The rest is close. Dad helped me build the desk."

"I have a vivid picture of it."

"The bed wasn't what you're imagining though."

I hear the grin seep into Ben's voice. "How did you know I was thinking about your bed?"

I bark a laugh. "Call it a lucky guess."

"What was it? Canopied?"

"A bunk bed." My answer has him watching me with rapt curiosity. "I shared a room with my brother."

Ben's brows lift. "You have a brother?"

My throat tightens. "An older one."

"Not so close?" he asks tentatively.

My fingers bore into the mattress at my sides. "We were as kids. We used to mess around in the bush. We built a treehouse together. Dug caves."

"And now?" His voice sounds quiet and tight, like he's holding his breath.

I watch the shadows of branches from the pohutakawa tree sway against the ceiling. "Now we're not so close. Not in contact at all."

"Jack . . ."

Ben shifts, the mattress dips, and he crosses right over that humming line. I shut my eyes, but I feel him looking down at me.

My heart bangs against my chest. It wars inside me to curl a hand around his neck and crush him into a kiss. But the ache of memories keeps me rooted to the bed.

Slowly, I reopen my eyes.

He's watching me. His Adam's apple bulges on a swallow.

He speaks slowly, an uncertain waver in his voice. "Are you in contact with any of your family?"

My chest rises with a sharp, aching breath. "No."

"Is it because—"

"Yes."

"They cut you out of their lives?"

"When I came out on my twenty-second birthday." When no amount of gestures made them accept my "choice." I'll never forget that sorrowful look from my older brother, before he picked up his bible and headed to the Kingdom Hall.

Ben's breath sighs over my cheek. His sorrow is a huge, pained depth in his eyes. "You know."

"Know?" I croak.

"What it's like to have your family ripped away."

We stare at each other. I read his pain and he reads mine. Neither of us speaks for a long time. Shadows dance on the ceiling and we let it distract us.

"It hurts," he whispers later.

"Yes." I can barely get the word out of my tight throat.

His pinkie bumps mine and a pocket of air puffs the blanket as he hovers his hand over mine. The pads of his fingers bump against my fingernails. He's waiting for me to say this is okay.

I freeze.

The dance of his fingertips over mine feels intimate.

His trembling breath snags in my chest. He draws away, and I lift my hand and capture his fingers between mine. His palm clamps to the back of my hand. His breath stutters much like my own.

I squeeze our fingers.

Chapter Twenty-Four

BEN

A RAINBOW STREAMS INTO THE BEDROOM.

That's how I know something's weird about this morning.

I stretch, fingers pressing against the headboard, thigh muscles pulling, morning wood dragging under the sheets.

Jack has left the bed and there's a ruckus in the living room.

It's weird, because I'm usually awake before the sun and I'm always the first person out of bed in the cottage.

I fish for my phone on the nightstand. Eight in the morning?

Holy shit. I must have slept like a stone.

I haven't slept through like that since . . . a long time.

I check my messages and immediately wish I hadn't. My manager has asked if, along with Monday to Wednesday, I'll do a half day on Thursday before my vacation kicks in.

It reminds me that Milo will hate spending a week of his school holiday lounging around the museum.

I close my eyes and listen to Jack barking in the background. Such a great, authoritative voice.

There's an idea. Maybe Jack wouldn't mind babysitting this week?

I stumble out of bed, the shock of cool floor biting into my heels. I haul myself to the bathroom, and on the way out, I veer toward a frustrated sounding Jack.

I steal inside the doorway. Back to me, Jack is pacing the width of the living room in a white tank top and butt-hugging jeans. "Thank you very much."

On that grumpy note, he ends his call, shoves his phone in his back pocket, and jerks around with the darkest frown I've seen on him.

He sees me and startles. "When did you sneak in here?"

"Between Christ-in-a-handbasket and Lucifer's trident up someone's ass." I shake my head. "Here I thought you old guys had it all together."

Jack raises a dangerous brow. "Old guys?"

"Mature." He prowls closer, and I like the glint in his eyes. His gaze zips down my almost naked body. My toes curl against the slats, and I continue, "Like a ripe cheese. You know, it gets better with age."

"Cheese?" He's past the halfway point and my veins skip with anticipation.

Jack's impatience tingles in my cock. The wallpaper is bumpy at my back and the air is fraught with static. My pecs and nipples are hard. I swallow, and keep teasing, "Not plain colby or anything. Tasty. The good stuff."

Two feet. "I'm not sure if this is the best insult I've heard, or the worst come-on."

"Come-on, definitely. I like cheese."

He stops, his socked feet an inch from my bare ones. "All cheese?"

"The vintage stuff." It takes Herculean effort for him not to lean in closer. If I reach out, I think he might fold.

This time, I'm the one who must perform hero-like resistance. Jack doesn't really want this, he's just in a mood. I shouldn't take advantage of it.

I should do the adult thing.

God I hate the adult thing.

I sidle away and focus on the chair Jack likes to read on. "What were you cursing about?"

He takes a moment, but when he speaks, he sounds like he's in control again. In control, and relieved nothing just happened. "The walls between this room, the master bedroom, and the kitchen. They aren't load bearing ones, but it seems like permissions are still going to be a pain in the ass. We might be looking at four to six weeks. I'd hoped to be done before summer."

"Because of your villa?" My voice drops. He's leaving soon to buy his dream home. Of course he is. This was always supposed to be temporary.

I swallow the achy disappointment.

"I gotta buckle down and finish the renovations," Jack says. "We should shop for your kitchen, too."

Kitchen. Right.

All I hear is that he won't have time to play babysitter this week.

"So, how long will it take once we choose a kitchen and have permissions?"

"The actual remodeling shouldn't take more than a week."

I frown. "Oh. That's . . . soon."

Milo stumbles into the lounge, yanking on a T-shirt. "Devansh just called," he says. "He invited me to a Weta Workshop tour with him and his dad. Can I go?"

"Good morning to you, too," I say.

"Morning fantail. Morning woodpecker."

Jack rolls his eyes.

"Can I?" Milo asks in full-on puppy mode.

As if I'd say no to free time. "Sure. Um, let me get dressed first."

His brow furrows. He swings his head to Jack and back. "Hold it. Did I walk in on something?"

"No!" I yelp. "Jack's your *teacher*. This here" —I wave a hand between clothed Jack and practically naked me—"it's all platonic. One hundred percent. Two hundred, even. You know what, let's go all the way to one thousand percent."

Milo lifts his eyebrows. "You sound weird, Ben."

"I do not!" My voice strains at the end. I clear my throat. "I do not. Now hurry up and get ready before I change my mind."

Milo spins to Jack. "What did you do to my brother? He's broken."

Amusement sparkles in Jack's eyes. "I think Milo means you're the one who needs to get ready."

I follow their gazes and fold my arms. "Of course, I know that." I stomp out of the room. "And I'm not broken. I just . . . overslept."

Five minutes later, I am dressed in jeans and one of Jack's soft T-shirts that loosely hugs my chest. Jack, shoving on a flannel shirt at the front door, notices, but I spare him a look not to say anything. "I wasn't thinking clearly about what I needed last night."

At the mention of last night, the air suddenly stills between us. Our gazes snag.

The warmth of his hand echoes in my palm.

Tenderness pulses into me.

Jack's chest expands as if he's breathing it in too.

The intensity is too sharp and sudden.

I break away from it and shove my shoes on. He abruptly jingles his keys and calls to Milo, who is banging about in his bedroom for his Pokémon cards.

Hold up. Jack is all ready to go, a gray beanie stuffed into his back pocket. "I thought I was driving Milo?"

"We need to head to the supermarket. I thought we could combine things?" He throws me his keys and I catch them against my navel. "You can drive if you like."

I rub the metal key to the truck. "I mean, I *love* to drive as much as I love being . . . driven. I just don't love to drive actual vehicles if someone else is offering."

Jack snorts. "Christ. Give me those keys back."

~

AFTER DROPPING MILO OFF AT HIS FRIEND'S, WE HEAD TO NEW World supermarket. We both grab carts, then awkwardly look at each other.

Jack pauses and returns his to the rack. He returns confidently. "What do you think of us cooking together this week?"

My belly gives an involuntary skip. "For our health?"

"And to save on dinner dishes and scheduling time for the kitchen."

I snicker. "Yeah, all those microwave meals take forever to prepare. And the dishes . . ."

He bumps me away from the cart and takes over wheeling it. "Smart ass."

The stupid grin at my face stretches into a smile. "Okay, you head straight to the meat counter and queue up before the lines hit."

"Lines?"

"Talia says it's in my mind, but whenever I come here, there's always a long ass line for meat."

He laughs. "Never noticed."

"So have fun. I'll meet you there with some basics."

Before he can reply, I dash off into the supermarket and pluck groceries off shelves.

At the meat counter, Jack is plopping fresh steaks into the cart. He doesn't even look up to know I'm there.

"You better be holding something green in your arms," he says.

Um . . . "I'm an idiot. I do have a block of vintage cheese, if that counts?"

"Drop it in the cart. Let's grab some spinach and mushrooms."

My lips twist in distaste as I lower the food into the cart by a family-sized box of Weet-Bix. My tongue sticks to the roof of my mouth seeing that large box. "Spinach, cool. What about Brussels sprouts? Or cauliflower?"

"You don't like mushrooms?"

"There's only one mushroom-shaped thing I—"

"Cauliflower's fine."

I sidle to Jack's side and it's my turn to bump him to the side. I push the cart away. Jack gives me a nervous glance at my controlling the cart, and I shake my head. "No soft drinks while we're under the same roof, I promise."

I don't know what the hell possessed me to say that, but Jack's relieved grin makes it worth it.

Also, if I give a little here, maybe Jack will give a little, too? Maybe he won't feel quite so busy and want to look after Milo even one of the days I'm working?

"Tuna," he says.

"Sure, how much?" The end of my car thumps against something metallic. I whip my head toward a wall of bloody tuna. It's wobbling.

For fuck's sake. Again?

I lunge forward. Behind me, Jack's laugh booms down the aisle.

I bathe in the electrical dance tickling my nape. His hand closes next to mine on the handle. "How about instead of darting off and grabbing things separately, we do it together?"

I rub my nape. "I'd like to do things together. Now. This whole week."

"Whole week?"

"I'll pay you, of course."

He frowns. "Pay me for what?"

"It's just with school holidays . . . I'm not sure how to manage with Milo. And I thought, since you have a break too, maybe you could look after him sometimes—"

"Sure," Jack says.

"—Not all the time. I don't want to steal into your plans. But I have to work and he's bored of spending hours at Te Papa, and I know it's a lot to ask—"

"I'll do it," Jack says.

"—I'll make it up to you of course, and financially. Totally. Name your price. And if he gets too much, you can change your mind at any time, and—"

Jack plants a hand atop mine, staying the cart I've started pushing.

His calloused fingers rub over my knuckles. "I'd love to look after Milo." He holds my gaze. "I have a few smaller house projects he can help me with, and I have a soccer game with Jeremy and Luke that Milo is welcome to join."

Sob-like gratitude bubbles up my throat. "Really?"

"One stipulation."

I nod. "Of course, anything."

He slides his off mine slowly. "No paying me to do it."

"But—"

He looks at me tightly. There's no fighting this, and I don't want to.

"Okay. I won't pay you."

"Good."

"Good?"

"Good."

"Good." My belly is one hundred, two hundred, one thousand percent butterflies.

Chapter Twenty-Five

JACK

"Do you think if I'm really good for you, Ben might get me a puppy?"

I snort. "Not gonna happen. The puppy part. You're gonna be good though. Best behavior ever."

Milo narrows his eyes mischievously over the table where we've eaten lunch. "Or what?"

Ben wasn't wrong when he said kids hold all the power, Jesus.

Keeping kids in line in hourly increments is a whole different ball game to intensively spending days with one kid. Especially when that one kid is as quick-witted as Milo McCormick.

I swipe Milo's phone. "I'm keeping this hostage."

"What?" Milo says, unsure whether to laugh. "But I haven't done anything."

"Now you won't."

He folds his arms huffily. "Well played, Woodpecker."

After washing up, we head back into his bedroom to replace his rotting windowsill. We've removed the inner window from the pane and carefully pried the old sill off. Milo helps trace the measurements onto a piece of treated lumber and we saw a new sill.

"Slide this into place like this," I say, "and now it's time for the galvanized nails."

"You're good at this stuff," Milo says. "Ben hates changing lightbulbs."

I level him a look. "None of that while Ben's not here to defend himself."

"What? But it's true. He thinks he'll electrocute himself."

Curiosity pulls my gaze to the dangling light bulb. "Does he switch off the main electricity?"

Milo nods. "I'm not saying his fear makes sense. I'm saying he's an idiot."

"Your brother is a smart guy."

"Smart ass, maybe."

I pin him with a teacher look. "If you can't say something nice, say nothing. Let's finish securing the sill."

I hammer the nails into the frame and caulk the gaps. Milo stays pointedly quiet.

I dust my hands after I've finished propping the window in place. "Really? You have nothing nice to say about your brother?"

His eyes light up like it's a big joke. He presses his lips together and shakes his head.

"Come on," I say. "There are a thousand nice things you could say about Ben. He's the best."

He raises his brows.

"Admit I'm right, Milo."

He giggles, cheekily.

I get the ball rolling. "Ben is the best because he calls you bucko even if you piss him off. Ben is the best because there are always sparks of fun in his eyes when he looks at you. Ben is the best because he brags about you every chance he gets. Still nothing? You're going to make me work for it, aren't you?"

Milo nods.

We clean up our tools, and I'm determined to crack Milo into admitting the truth about how much he loves his brother. "Ben is the best because he's passionate about birds and stuff." The 'and stuff' almost breaks Milo's silence, but he bites back a rebuke for my bird ignorance. "Ben is the best because he never fails to smuggle you the last piece of chocolate. Ben is the best because he's so naturally giving."

An hour later while we're trucking to the park, I'm still working Milo.

It's drizzling but the rain isn't heavy enough to deter us. We jog around the soggy grass to warm up.

After we've stretched, I lightly bounce the ball off his head. "Ben is the best because even though his room in the cottage is a mess, he respects everyone else's spaces and keeps them clean."

We practice taking goal shots and I give Milo some tips. He's a quick learner. A little guidance and this boy could excel at the game.

"Ben is the best because he is always on your side—unless he's on mine, and then he's even better—"

Milo plants his hands on his hips and shakes his head.

I laugh. "I could continue for hours, you know."

He steps on the ball and looks at me. "Do."

"Ben is the best because he's always fondly messing your hair. Or nervously wrecking his own. He's the best because he knows he isn't perfect, but he damn well keeps trying to be better. He simply lights up every room he steps into and every person he meets."

I steal the ball from under Milo's foot and kick it into the goal. "Ben is the best because he tries to plan secret trips for you, and when they don't work, he feels like his world is falling apart. But mostly, Ben is the best because he plans his whole future around yours . . ."

I trail off. Milo's blinking rapidly, eyes watery.

The emotion on his face crushes me. This boy has so much love for Ben. I didn't actually need to hear him admit it, and yet I went too far. "Milo?"

He twists away from me.

I scoop up the cold, dirty ball and hug it under one arm. I settle a hand on his shoulder. "I'm sorry. I should have stopped."

He lifts his chin. His lip wobbles. "Ben is the . . . the . . ."

His shoulders curve and he jolts with silent sobs. I drop the ball and pull him into a hug. "Yeah. He is."

Milo hugs me back, then draws back, wiping a runny nose and sniffing. "He really tried surprising me with a trip?"

"I probably shouldn't have said that."

"Where did he want to take me?" He looks up at me. "No, don't tell me." He smiles. "I think I know."

"You do?"

"Kapiti Island. I told him I wanted to go there."

"I'm sure he'll take you again sometime."

Milo reaches for the ball and kicks it up on his knee. He catches it and his brow creases. "Jack?"

"Yeah?"

"Ben isn't working Thursday and Friday next week."

I suck in a breath. I know what's coming, and I know saying yes would have me inching over the line.

"Maybe we could surprise him?"

Chapter Twenty-Six

BEN

As soon as I'm off work, I head home, ready to bum around with the boys.

No one's home.

I slouch through the house. Over the last two weeks, Jack has recruited Milo to help him with renovations. Today they cleared the living room, stripped wallpaper from the walls, and painted sample squares of color next to the door

I run my finger down the gritty surface next to the samples. Eggshell was Jack and Milo's favorite, while mine was honey topaz. I think they had the better eye. Eggshell looks subtle and sophisticated.

I want to find the boys and tell them that they were right.

I want Jack to take me kitchen shopping like he's been encouraging me to do, not so I can see what I like, but so I can see what he does.

I send off a message.

Ben: *Where are you guys?*

I want Jack to know I miss them. Want to thank him for everything he's done for Milo. Want to work on the house together. Hang out after, too.

Fish 'n' chips overlooking the beach. We three in the truck, licking our salty fingers between grins. Or at home, over homemade chicken curry, while I negotiate how much it'll cost for Milo to quit looking at his phone until Jack confiscates it using his teacher-y ways.

He's my fucking hero.

I hope he's not tiring of us.

He looked wrecked this morning. Sleeping on the thin, bumpy rollout we borrowed from Luke our second night in the main house might have something to do with that. I tried switching places with him multiple times, but he wouldn't have it.

Maybe I should tackle him to the bed and pin him down until he agrees to stay. Tonight. Tomorrow night. All the nights.

I pull Johnathan Livingston's cord and plunk onto Jack's neatly made mattress.

I want to beat the thing up for having to be there at all.

But at least it's in my room where Jack offered to set it up. He'd gulped hard when I asked him to stay in here, but he understood. Being in this house comes with aches and, sometimes, panic attacks. Nothing I want to deal with alone. Nothing I want to impose on my brother.

My phone buzzes and I leap to my feet like the boys might be home, but it's just me and Johnathan.

I read Jack's message. They're at the local park playing soccer with a few guys.

I'm already out the door.

It's cold and wet outside, but the rain has ceased. Good

enough weather for a walk. Good enough weather to fix the cottage roof.

I shiver in the sunshine peeking through the clouds.

Fifteen minutes later, I'm at the park gazing over a muddy area that might have been grass a week ago. A group of boys soars across the field flocking to the goal.

I stand at the sidelines—what I guess are the sidelines—and take stock of the guys hustling after a ball. Milo is the shortest and he's running blindly after a lanky teenager up the wing. Luke, who I've spotted a few times on school grounds, is bouncing on the balls of his feet between the goalposts. I am positive the guy rubbing his freezing arms at the other wing is Luke's partner Sam. Positive because the only other adult aside from Jack on the field is Kresley's newest teacher Mr. Campbell.

Mr. Campbell can play. He weaves the ball like it's an extension of himself.

Jack jostles him for the ball. He's wearing sneakers, Nike sports pants, and a long-sleeved T-shirt with the sleeves shoved mid-forearm. Sweat seeps into the V, and his muscles shine and flex with every running step.

Jack squares off against Mr. Campbell, grinning. He says something, and Mr. Campbell laughs and pretends to hold the ball hostage. He doesn't even try to stop Jack.

I know exactly what the guy's doing. He's about one phone-number away from sending Jack a dick pic.

Sometimes it sucks to be fluent in flirt.

I shouldn't have come.

I slink back a step. Maybe I can escape unseen?

My damn bucko screeches my name.

I freeze, and Jack whips his head up. A surprised smile bursts across his face. He steps on the ball, halting it, and waves me onto the field.

I look behind me, hoping he's gesturing to some other soccer lover.

"Ben," he calls out. "Come, join in."

"You have even teams. I better not."

Luke and the others chime in that I'm welcome to jump in. I don't think they know how quickly puffed I get.

Jack leaves the ball and jogs over. "You can join my team."

"From that I take you are not in it to win it."

He laughs. "Milo is pretty damn good. So is Luke. We're a solid team."

"Oh, so you want to even up the playing field?"

"You can't be that bad."

Over his shoulder, I spot Sam dodging an oncoming ball. "Okay, maybe not that bad. But there are no hat tricks here."

His laugh fuels me with energy and I follow him onto the stodgy field.

My soles slurp into the ground, and I spend ten minutes happily watching the guys play.

Mr. Campbell lets Jack sneak the ball from him again and again, and each time my vision doubles. Milo sneaks up to me and delivers a stinging slap on the back. "See those white poles all the way down there?"

"You mean our goal?"

"Oh, so you do know what it is."

"You are so showering and washing your hair tonight and I'm not paying you a cent to do it."

Milo laughs and jogs away.

"I mean it," I call after him. "I'll stick Jack on you."

He turns around jogging backwards. "Good luck. Jack's going out tonight."

He's going out? I snap my head toward Mr. Campbell.

Look at him, with his fancy soccer shoes and club T-shirt focusing on nothing except the ball or Jack.

Mr. Campbell dribbles toward the goal, and I realize I'm standing between him and his goal.

Great. An opportunity to show off just how brilliantly inadequate I am against this man.

Ah, fuck it. I jog toward the ball. Jack closes in behind Mr. Campbell, eyes trained on us.

Don't flinch. Just kick the ball away. That's all.

I slip and slide in a thick patch of mud. I swing my foot for the ball—

Mr. Campbell taps it around me and disappears.

"Fuck," I mutter, and then mutter again as Jack and I wallop into each other. I clutch handfuls of his shirt for balance. I know what's about to happen a second before it happens.

Our gazes clash, and Jack curses as I lose my balance. I yank him down with me as my legs slide between his.

The ground slurps me into it, squishy and cold. Weight crushes against me and robs my lungs of air. Jack is plastered on me, chest to my heart-pounding chest, thigh to my crotch, and hands splayed in the mud either side of my shoulders. His fingers sink through mud, and our noses bump.

"Deja'vu 2.0," I breathe.

A humored murmur, "What?"

Around us, cheers lift in the air as Mr. Campbell presumably scores.

I'm marginally annoyed I didn't stop the guy scoring, but it's impossible to keep up an angry heat with Jack softly puffing over my cheek and top lip.

"Reminds me of the first day we met," I say.

Jack squirms against me as he tries to find purchase in the mud.

"Only this fall is *significantly* better."

He laughs and curses.

"I'm glad you convinced me to play after all."

He stops moving and scowls at me, but I don't miss the crinkling at the edges of his eyes. There's a speck of mud on Jack's cheek, just under his eye. His beard combs the inside of my wrist as I try to wipe it off him.

I make it worse, smearing mud on his skin.

My laugh rumbles through us like a warm friction.

"You guys all right there?" Mr. Campbell asks.

Moment over.

My laugh dies and a horrible weight plunges into my belly.

Jack pushes onto his knees, and I sit up. I clutch one of his quads either side of my thighs, and his eyes shoot to mine. "Is it true? Are you going out tonight?"

Before he can answer, Mr. Campbell offers Jack a hand up.

I lunge for Mr. Campbell's hand so Jack doesn't. As I pull to my feet, my grip might be tighter than warranted.

Jack chuckles behind me, and Mr. Campbell gives me a shrewd look.

I grin. "Mr. Campbell, right?"

"Like the soup," he answers.

"You're good," I say. "But don't think you're going to score again today."

When I turn around, Jack is shaking his head.

Fifteen minutes later, the sky opens and rain buckets down.

I've never been so happy for wet weather.

Milo and Jack grab their equipment and, with hurried goodbyes, we leave the park.

We track muddy water through the house as we chase each other inside. Milo hides in his bedroom to avoid showering as long as possible, and Jack jumps in first.

I strip out of my mud-caked clothes and shove them into

the washing machine along with Milo and Jack's gear. Shivering in my underwear, I turn on a load, then dash through the house.

Steam sifts out from the gap in the bathroom door, and I pause when I hear Jack singing. I grin when I make out the lyrics. Phil Collins. "You Can't Hurry Love."

Why yes, that would seem to be true . . .

The drumming of water snaps off and I lurch my chilled limbs to the bedroom.

Fuck, I'm out of clean clothes in the main house. I could have sworn I had one pair of jeans lying around. As much as I'd like to jump into Jack's, his pants will fall off me.

I open my childhood drawers. Nothing. Nothing. Nothing. My old dragon-boating uniform from when I was sixteen. Nothing.

Crap.

Maybe when I folded washing, I accidentally put my jeans on Milo's pile?

I am about to enter his room when I see him hunched over on his bed, phone to his ear and giggling. The sweet, innocent giggle tempts me to listen in.

"Yeah, but she's nothing to Kora."

Kora?

I'm glued to the doorframe.

"I like her face and her tits are big. She said she wants to go out with me."

I peel away from the doorframe and breath wheezes out of my lungs. He's eleven! That's . . . that's too young, right?

But aren't kids trying things younger and younger these days?

Last month I read about a twelve-year-old girl giving birth.

How much have I prepped Milo for these things?

Oh fuck, fuck.

I need clothes. I need . . . stuff to explain other stuff.

I don't have stuff.

Maybe Jack has stuff.

I can't use Jack's stuff!

I'm back in my bedroom. I yank something on, grab my wallet and phone, and fling on my parka. The damn zip won't cooperate.

I jam my feet into my shoes without socks.

"Ben?" Jack's voice trails down the hall. "You off somewhere?"

"I gotta . . . There's stuff I gotta . . ."

I gotta race around the corner to the mall for *things*.

I launch myself outside.

Rain pounds over my head and drizzles down my legs and under the neck of my parka. I splash through puddles, fingers numb as I try calling Talia. Once. Twice.

All I get is the stupid voicemail.

Vaguely, in the distance, I hear a shout.

I drip my way into the supermarket, right to the aisle I need. I grab stuff off the shelf.

"Ben?"

I lurch around. "Jack?"

He's pulling a wet beanie off his shower-damp hair. Rainwater rolls off the sleeves of his jacket. He must have jogged after me.

His frown oscillates between worried and puzzled. "What's going on?"

I give a strangled laugh. "This kid business is awkward, awkward, awkward."

"Awkward, okay."

His relief shifts to surprise as my parka parts and he sweeps a long glance down my length.

"What?" I follow his gaze and take in my dragon-boating uniform with its ultra-short shorts and shrink-wrapped top.

Jack starts to chuckle.

"I had nothing else."

He hides his smirk and nods to the boxes I'm strangling. "Dare I ask what's got you so agitated?"

"Remind me once Milo's grown up and left the house never to have kids of my own. It's all silent treatment and uncomfortable conversations and excessive worry—which, let me tell you, is starting to have an effect on my hair."

"It's falling out?"

"Prematurely whitening."

"Tell you what. I'll remind you that you don't want kids if you explain what's going on." Jack gestures to the box in my hand. "And how a fertility test will help."

I slide the box onto the shelf like a hot potato. Heat prickles down my neck where Jack's watching me with patient curiosity.

"He likes Kora. A girl at school, and I'm pretty sure he knows the birds and the bees basics but does he really? What about condoms, safe sex, and safe words?"

Jack starts to interject, but I cut him off. "I don't know how much he knows about girls and their systems—and crap, neither do I. And Talia isn't answering her phone—"

Jack lays his hands on my wet shoulders with a firm squeeze and steers me to look at him. He's smiling softly. "That was more than I bargained for."

"Join the club. What do I do, Jack?"

His eyes are dancing. "Come get coffee with me."

"Coffee?"

He gently steers me to the checkout and stays by my side as I pay for the Trojans. I stuff the box awkwardly into my pocket, and sigh.

Jack takes my hand with a comforting squeeze, and doesn't let go until the warmth of the nearest café cocoons us.

Chapter Twenty-Seven

JACK

WE SIT AT A ROUNDED TABLE IN THE CORNER OF THE CAFÉ, cappuccinos planted before us. The music in here fades into the background and doesn't hide the *snick*ing of Ben's sneaker sole against the tiles as he bounces his leg. Ben sips his drink and cradles the cup to his chest.

"I didn't mean for you to worry and chase after me," he says. "I'll calm down before I chat with him."

I rub the dented surface of the table as I search for a way to lessen his worry. "He has a crush on a girl."

"Did you think I forgot? That was the whole point of the condoms." His brow creases. "We should get home so I can give him the talk."

"Maybe you're overreacting to this?"

"Should I be underreacting?"

"No, that's not what I meant. Just, take a breath."

"God I wish I could navigate life as calmly as you." He sighs. "I'm being stupid, aren't I?"

"You're concerned. That is completely understandable."

"It is?"

"Yeah. Can I say something?"

Ben nods, then interrupts—"Oh my God. I just ran out and left Milo at home."

This guy. How did I ever not have him in my life? "We're talking twenty minutes here. I told him to watch something on Netflix until we get back. It's okay."

He sinks back in his chair, coffee sloshing onto the tight T-shirt that will haunt all my dreams. "Sorry. What did you want to say?"

"You are doing a great job. You are caring and enthusiastic about giving Milo the best you can. Every day, I am more and more impressed when I see you together. I'm touched by your bond. Milo is the luckiest kid to have you as an older brother."

"But?"

"Hang on a sec, don't dismiss those words so quickly."

"They feel like puffer to a big 'but'."

"Not a big 'but'."

"A small one, then?"

"Ben!" I laugh out my exasperation. "I'm worried about you."

"Me?"

"You are stressing yourself out."

"I'm fine."

"You dashed out in a storm wearing dragon-boating gear."

"And a parka." He wrings out a knowing sigh. "You think I should let go of the fear he gets a girl pregnant?"

"The sex-ed conversation is important. But it's a crush. All those butterflies and shyness. Don't you remember how special it is?"

Ben's gaze smacks mine. "It's special all right. Every time you look at them, your heart skips a beat. Every time they come close, your skin dances with a shiver. Every time they smile, you melt, and every time you speak, you make a fool of yourself."

I lean in, swallowing the lump in my throat because I know I'm crossing the line. I whisper, "You've never made a fool of yourself to me, Ben."

His cheeks brighten, but he doesn't look away. He swallows. "Do you remember your first crush?"

"I'll never forget."

"Share it with me?"

I rub over bits of sugar on the table. "I was camping with my brother and dad in the Wairarapa. There was a boy across the camping grounds, close to the river. He got up every morning, jogged, and stretched outside his tent. I'd skip stones as close as I could and admire his lithe, sweat-slickened body as he bent and flexed. I'll always remember the jerking in my belly when he caught me staring. I couldn't take my eyes off him, and I was afraid, and then he smiled and I floated."

"Did you ever learn his name?"

"We met again two summers later. I was almost sixteen. His name was Adam and he was one year older."

Ben hunches forward. "What happened?"

I gulp my coffee. "You know, perhaps we should head back."

"Jack, you're blushing. If you don't tell me, my mind will wander."

"He became my first. There, at the edge of the river. It hurt like a son-of-a-bitch, but his smile made it worth it."

Ben's eyes narrow much like they did with Mort on the field. "I wanted to know, but I wish I didn't ask."

"So we both have firsts?"

Ben tugs his ear, staring across the café with quick glances at me. "Mine hurt too. I almost asked him to stop. He was careful and kind, and it got better."

Yep. Harder to hear than I thought. I drain my coffee of its last dredge. "I'm glad he was kind," I grind out.

"It was what I liked most about him. What I like most." Ben leans forward. "A guy who is kind. Good. Solid."

Our knees knock under the table. "Shall we bring back a ginger slice for Milo?"

He nods but doesn't move to stand. "Jack?"

"Yes?"

"Thank you for everything. Saving us from the leaky roof, helping me out these last couple of weeks with Milo, and calming me now."

"You're welcome."

I drag my chair back—

"Also, eggshell," he says.

I stay seated and the little flicker of relief over Ben's face tells me he doesn't want this moment to end.

Neither do I.

"Eggshell?" I ask.

"It's a perfect color for the walls."

I search the bottom of my cup like my future might be told there. I know I'll regret it if I cut this moment short. "Ben, would you like another coffee with me?"

He bites his lip. "Aren't you going out tonight? Soon?"

I pull out my phone.

"What are you doing?" he asks as I lift the phone to my ear.

It rings twice. "Luke," I say, staring at Ben. "Thanks for inviting me to dinner tonight, but"—I putter out a cough—"I'm coming down with something. Can we do a rain check?"

When I hang up, Ben lips hitch at the sides. "You weren't going out with Mr. Campbell?"

"I'm not interested in him."

Ben springs up and twists toward the counter, but not before I catch his dazzling smile. He returns—face amusedly schooled—with more coffee and a slice to take back to Milo.

We hop from subject to subject until our drinks are done and it's time to move on.

"You're right," he says as we vacate the table. "Crushes are special. I remember Mum and Dad teasing me mercilessly about a girl I liked—the only girl, incidentally. They're fond memories." Ben opens the door for me. "I'd like Milo to have such memories, too. Would you gently rib him with me?"

My step stutters on the threshold. "Like your mum and dad did?"

He nods.

My belly jerks a hundred times harder than watching my first crush smile. My veins sing as I stumble into the storm.

I tug Ben's hand and pull him toward me.

The café sign on the door flaps wildly. A trolley bus slows to a stop at the curb, and people rush off and on. Someone whistles to a dog across the street.

Ben's cheeks are flushed, and he tucks his free hand under his armpit. I step forward to block the wind from him. He licks his lips and smirks. "What are you doing, Jack?"

I draw out my beanie from my back pocket and slip it on his head, tucking his ears inside.

He loses his smirk, and his eyes dart to mine, blazing.

My voice comes out thick and unsteady. "Let's make Milo some memories."

Chapter Twenty-Eight

BEN

I wake up wanting to repeat last night.

Not the retreating to our separate bed-slash-mattress part, but the hours before that. When Jack and I traded grins over schnitzel and mashed potato while teasing Milo about this girl Kora.

I loved how red Milo turned as he tried denying it.

Loved the glares that wobbled into giggles.

Loved how dramatically he folded his arms and huffed from the room in an urgent need to call Devansh.

I'm pretty sure he's plotting revenge against me.

Make that very sure.

Milo has a cunning smirk this morning.

I should probably cool off ribbing Milo. It might bite me in the ass.

I like Jack's growing ease around me. The touches to my

arm and the casual bumping of our hips as we fight for the coffeepot.

I'm nervous about my brother bringing this new comfort to Jack's attention. Nervous Jack might stop.

Milo slurps the last of the milk from his bowl of Weet-Bix and pins Jack with a determined look. I foresee words tumbling out of his mouth.

I leap to my feet, knocking over my bowl.

"Milo!"

He casts me a puzzled frown, while Jack picks up our bowls and disappears into the kitchen. "What?" Milo asks.

"Let's go, um, for a walk."

"No can do, Ben."

Jack returns behind me, a hovering warmth, and Milo's grin explodes.

"Go. Go. Go," Milo yells.

Jack spins me around and heaves me over his shoulder. My lungs expel a surprised burst of air. I scrabble for purchase, pushing myself on Jack's hips. "What?"

Jack claps the back of my thighs and grunts as he chases Milo out the house.

Startled, I laugh and yelp. "Jack, what are you doing?"

At his truck, he slides me off him. His hands burn through my shirt to my side and the curve of my ass. I hit the pavement and gasp for breath.

His laughter tickles my freshly shaven jaw, and behind us Milo's sneakers smack through puddles. Jack doesn't move back. There's a few inches between us—inches that a month ago he'd have widened. But not today.

Milo plows between us and opens the passenger door. He slides inside.

Jack smiles at me and heads around the truck to the driver's side.

Milo waves a chocolate bar. "Jump in, Ben."

I heave myself into the passenger seat. "What's going on?"

Milo hands me the chocolate. "We're off to Kapiti Island."

"What? Really? Why?"

Jack starts the ignition and pointedly nudges Milo.

"Oh, um," my brother shrugs. "Because you're tired and need a break."

Jack shakes his head and sighs deeply. "Four tiny words, Milo. Three if you use a contraction. We practiced this."

"You practiced more than I did. You say them."

I skip my gaze from Jack to Milo and back again. "Someone say them."

They speak at the same time, the exact same words. "You're the best."

Forget driving to the Kapiti Coast.

I drift there on a daydream.

I KEEP BRUSHING UP AGAINST JACK. HE HASN'T SEEMED TO notice how frequent these touches are, or how deliberate, but I'm cataloguing each one. I'm a junkie for the little sparks that fly between us, and I'm after a harder hit.

I'm also after a bloody good excuse to share the double bed in the deluxe tent he and Milo rented.

Of course, the assumption is Milo and I share the big bed and Jack takes the small one, but if I can manipulate the situation to look totally innocent and platonic between Milo's teacher and me sharing the double, I'm going to find it.

"Ben?" Jack whispers, close to my ear.

"Hmm?"

"Do you see the kiwi stumbling through the foliage?"

I jerk to my senses. It's twilight and we're at the beach. Purple light turns the leaves into silhouettes. It takes some adjusting before I spot the native bird. The kiwi shuffles over the ground, less than six feet away. It's a nicely rounded one with stout legs and brown, hair-like feathers. Its chopstick beak picks at the earth for grubs and worms. I hold my breath as it blindly veers toward us.

In the distance, water breaks against the shore, and salty breezes rustle through five finger and kanuka trees. Milo huddles close to my left, and the sleeve of Jack's coat combs mine.

My limbs are heavy from tramping every inch of the island, and my feet are burning. I could continue devouring the delights of this island all night.

Except for the part where I want to curl up close to Jack, in the same bed . . .

Our guide leads us back toward camp for dinner. Jack keeps glancing at me, and Milo drags behind.

"What?" I say.

"I thought you'd be first to spot the kiwi. Where were you back there?"

Yeah, not going to say. Unable to mask a grin, I swivel on my heel and address Milo. "How freaking awesome is this day?"

Milo tucks his hands under his armpits and nods.

Dinner is sweet potato and lamb stew. Jack is chatting with the guide. Milo stares at his bowl and barely eats a mouthful. I elbow him and murmur, "It's not Jack's, but it's not that bad."

He gives me a pithy chuckle. "Right."

At my urging, the three of us take another short walk before heading to our tent.

My mind has been racing through double-bed excuses.

Maybe I could tell Milo that Jack has a bad back and needs the better mattress. That Milo should take the single bed, and I'll, um, suck it up and crash with Jack.

I snort at myself, startling Jack.

"Nothing." I race into our tent and turn on the light rigged inside. "How about a game?"

Milo drops to the round rug and Jack digs out travel Scrabble from his backpack.

Milo excuses himself to the outhouse a dozen yards from the tent, and for the first time today it's just the two of us.

Jack tosses me the game and I catch it. He settles on the rug, sitting cross-legged opposite me. I pull out the board and tiny letters.

"Milo looks rosy today," Jack says, a hum in his voice.

"All the fresh air."

Jack focuses on the board. "He's quiet, too."

"Exhausted from all the walking. Hey, we should do this more often."

Jack hums a laugh and pulls seven letters from the sack. My mind skips from sack to *sack*, and being in the sack. With Jack.

I'm staring over his shoulder at the floral-sheeted bed when Milo flaps his way inside the tent. He rips out a burp. "Sorry."

"Oh my God, Jack. There's something wrong with him." I yank him down next to us. "He said *sorry*."

Milo groans at my poor joke.

My competitive side rears its head the moment Jack lays the word tummy on the board.

I scour my letters. "How bad is your back, Jack?"

Jack clears his throat. "Come again?"

I fiddle with an 'a' and a 'k' as Milo stares blatantly at my letters.

"I mean, you hefted me over your shoulder. It would be understandable if it threw your back out."

"It feels fine."

"Maybe you should take the big bed tonight. Make sure you're not aching tomorrow."

"Yeah, I don't think that would help any aching."

Maybe it's the light but I swear his gaze is glittery with a suppressed laugh.

"Yak," Milo says impatiently.

"Okay, I'm getting there." I set the letters on the board, and Jack suddenly moves.

A worried frown crushes his expression, and he's on his knees reaching toward Milo—

Milo vomits all down Jack's front. "Sorry, sorry," Milo garbles and stumbles to the edge of the tent and throws up again.

I'm moving before I've even processed what the hell just happened. I scooch to Milo and rub his heaving back. "Geez, Milo. Shit. You okay? I mean, get it out. Get it all out."

"Sorry—" he tries again, and I shake my head.

I'm the one who should be sorry. I should've seen it. Jack saw it, while I blindly ignored the signs, too caught up in myself. In what I wanted.

Fuck.

I want to kick myself. Dammit.

I set a trembling palm against Milo's forehead. He's burning up.

My instinct is to panic. I close my eyes and take a calming breath. Step by step. I've got this.

Jack is calmly stripping out of his clothes. He ducks into a fresh T-shirt.

"What can I do?" Concern and sincerity tinge his voice.

God, he's a kind man. No disgust that Milo threw up on him. No impatience waiting for an apology. He takes it in stride.

"Water bottle," I croak. "Do we have any ibuprofen?"

"He's feverish?"

"I think so."

"I'll hunt for Panadol."

He steps over a puddle of Milo's mess.

I wince. "I'll clean up soon."

He passes me a bottle of water and shoves on boots. "You focus on Milo, Ben. I've got this."

MILO THROWS UP IN BOUTS. HE DRAGGED HIMSELF TO THE outhouse and I followed carrying wet wipes and water.

I sit with my legs out the door, leaning against the inner wall. Milo rests on my lap, Jack's emergency sleeping bag spread over his legs. He murmurs thank you, over and over, as if he is a burden. It's crushing my heart.

I push the hair off his face, like mom did with mine when I was sick. I trace over the scar at his temple. "You know, it's kind of like we're married."

"If I hadn't just thrown up my entire insides, I'd throw up again."

I snicker. "Yeah, that was weird. But really, I take you as my brother for better, for worse, for richer, for poorer, in sickness and health, until death do us part."

He rolls his head and looks up at me for a long beat. "I do."

Movement outside catches my eye and I glance up to find Jack a few yards from us, smiling gently. Our gazes hold. Finally, he crosses to us.

"You both need sleep. Come back to the tent."

"What if I need to chuck again?" Milo says.

"I found a bucket. You can use that. If you miss, we'll clean up."

"It is kinda cold out here," Milo hedges.

I help him to his feet while Jack grabs the sleeping bag and water bottle.

Inside the tent, Milo hesitates. "Maybe I should sleep on the floor and you guys share."

I steer him to the double bed and help him under the covers.

"Are you sure?"

I settle in on the other side. "You're right where you're meant to be. And so am I."

Chapter Twenty-Nine

BEN

JACK HERE. LEAVE A MESSAGE AFTER THE, AH, TONE.

That little 'ah.' That moment of uncertainty—so real. I can't stop listening to it. Smiling at it.

It's the last Saturday of the school break and Jack's been out visiting Howie and his villa. Milo and I have bummed around all day playing video games.

It's only been four hours, but after two days of misadventure on Kapiti Island, it feels weird without Jack around.

Milo is sprawled on his clearly recovered belly, kicking his legs as he slays dragons on his phone. I'm draped over Jack's reading chair, one arm hooked behind my head, the other holding my phone to my ear. *"Jack here. Leave a message after the, ah, tone."*

Milo snickers. "I can hear it, by the way. That's how I know this is the seventh time you've called Jack without leaving a message."

I'd initially called to tell him the permissions came through for the kitchen renovation.

Would it really only take him a week to remodel?

And then what?

It took me three tries to leave a message.

"I'll see him tonight," I say to Milo. "It's not like I need to leave a message."

"Not like you need to hear his voice right now, either." He says with a teasing glint in his eye.

Yeah, it's definitely time to stop ribbing him about his crush . . .

Mumbling an excuse, I sneak off to the bedroom, and lying on Jack's mattress, I call him once more.

Jack here. . . The rest doesn't come, and—Fuck. "You answered?"

I sound panicked.

"I figured after seven missed calls I should. Are you okay?"

"I—" my voice cracks.

"Did something happen?" Jack's mistaken my incessant calls for an emergency.

"Um." Crap. I should tell him the truth. "Um. . ." But that makes me seem juvenile. Calling to hear his voice like a love-struck, stalking teenager.

I can't have him think of me that way.

What's something worthy of seven calls in a row? "I can't find Milo!"

Jack's tongue clicks. When he speaks, he's eerily calm. "What do you mean, you can't find him?"

I've overdone it. I need to scale back immediately. Come clean. "I mean, I said something and he ran away."

Fuuuuuck. I'm stupid. So stupid.

"I'm almost home."

I hang up. "Shit." I leap off the mattress and hunt down Milo.

He looks at me, startled. "What?"

Jack bursts into the kitchen where I'm pacing, a guilty panic riddling my bones. He tries to remain calm but there's a panicked urgency to his voice. "Here's the plan."

God, he's freaking out.

"I'll take the truck and head toward the park, and you—"

"Jack, stop." He doesn't hear me. He's still caught up in his worry for Milo. The sight socks me. I step in front of him.

"—head to the town belt. Did he take his binoculars?"

"Stop," I say again. Worry creases his brow and shame scalds my cheeks. "I lied. Milo didn't run away."

He halts, the words catching up to him. "What? Where is he?"

It feels like rocks are grinding in my stomach. "He ran away—but only because I told him to, because I told you that he had."

Jack raises his voice and his words break at the end. "What the hell are you talking about, Ben?"

Acid whips up my throat. I've fucked up badly this time. "He's fine. He's at the library."

He sags against the counter. "Christ. Why would you scare me like that?"

"It was stupid."

"You're damn right it was."

I hate being the cause of his tight frown and hard jaw. I've never seen him this upset. A part of me wants to make excuses, but that's not fair to Jack's feelings.

I struggle to speak, "My lie worried you, Jack. I'm deeply sorry to hurt you like that."

The fire in his eyes lessens. "It frightened me."

I want to take the whole stupid call back. I'm scared I've ruined something.

I want to hug him and apologize again. Want to beg him not to disappear out of our lives.

If I've ruined this, though, it's not just me who'll suffer the pain.

Oh God. Milo.

My throat feels tight. Like I'm breathing through a straw.

"Why have you gone so pale?" Jack asks, pushing off the counter. "What are you thinking?"

I can't even pretend to smile. To hide my feelings behind a joke.

My damn hands shake at my sides. "Forgive me, please."

My voice isn't mine. It's broken and gravelly.

Jack frowns, but only for a second before it melts again. Understanding shutters over his face.

One moment, he's standing three feet from me. The next, I'm folded into strong arms, his chest bumping against mine, his fingers pressing into my shoulder blades.

"You fucked up. I got angry. We fought." He pulls back enough for me to meet his earnest gaze and the serious set of his mouth. "It was just an argument." Jack crushes me tighter. "Oh, Christ, Ben."

"I'm really sorry."

"You're not perfect and neither am I. We'll fight again. I'll never just turn my back on you."

We sway together, one, two, three minutes. His beard presses against my ear. My nose bumps against the curve of his warm neck.

Comfortable. Reassuring.

He shivers when I let out a long breath of relief, and slowly extracts himself. "What do you say we grab Milo and do something together?"

I nod, and even though I don't like the reminder things will soon change, I want to be honest. Want to be a better adult.

I tell him that the permissions arrived today. "How about we hunt for a new kitchen?"

~

"YOU REALLY SHOULDN'T LISTEN TO ME WHEN I SUGGEST stupid things," I say to Milo as we head out of the library and scooch into Jack's truck.

"So I shouldn't listen at all then?"

I sigh. "Probably not."

Jack shakes his head and starts the car. "Are we ready for our mission?"

"Kitchens!" Milo acts as if we were heading to a theme park.

Our earlier argument is behind us, yet a thread of tenderness lingers. A reminder how easy it is to fuck up. "Ben?"

I nod.

Jack drives through town and every turn matches one in my gut. Jack dials down the music a few notches.

"What is the most common species of bird in the world?" Jack asks. "I'll give you a clue"—I snort, and his lips hitch—"it's delicious."

"Jack!" I laugh. "This is not how this game is played."

"Chicken," Milo says. "Oh, could we have that for dinner tonight?"

I have no words.

"Chicken cashew casserole?" Jack suggests.

"I'm turning vegetarian," I say.

"Give him a week," Milo says to Jack in hushed tones. "And he'll pluck the chicken himself."

I scowl. "I need Fanta."

Jack lifts a brow.

"What? I promised no drinking it while under the same roof. A promise I've kept."

"Barely."

"Drinking in the car outside the house doesn't break that oath."

"You're an addict."

"I live life by patterns, just like you, Mr. Phil Collins."

Jack throws me a baffled look. "What?"

"When you shower, you sing his songs."

"I do not."

Milo pipes in. "You do, Mr. Woodpecker. Ben has a theory you're making your way through his Best Of collection." I nudge Milo in the ribs to shut up, but he doesn't take the hint. "He's got a list."

Jack delightedly glances from Milo to me. "A list?"

"You'd think Ben has better things to do than hang outside the bathroom door and listen to you sing."

I inspect every millimeter of a scratch on the dashboard.

"Is that right?" Jack muses.

I snap the belt at my chest. "So like, other than the kitchen, what else needs to be done to the house?"

Thank fuck he rolls with the change in conversation. "The kitchen and interior painting are the last things to do inside. Then we've—you've—got to tidy up the yard."

You've. The weight of that correction sinks in my belly.

Jack continues, "In summer, you'll want a fresh coat of exterior paint."

I'd rather have Milo blurt out more embarrassing facts than continue this conversation.

"The kitchen warehouse!" Milo reads the sign cheerily as we enter the parking lot. "Let's do this."

The minute the truck is parked, Milo unsnaps his belt. I glare at the huge building for the obstacle it truly is. Stepping inside starts the countdown to Jack's imminent departure. Worse, brilliant sunshine glitters off the white façade.

There'll be no more putting off fixing the guest cottage. Whatever little time we have left won't be shared under the same roof.

"Move your butt," Milo says.

Jack is already out of the car and rounding to my side. He opens the door. "Coming?"

I perform my five-star cough again. "Maybe this was a bad idea after all. I don't want to spread germs. We should come back when I'm feeling better."

Milo shoves me out the door and Jack steadies me with a hand to my bicep. I reluctantly head inside to a world of kitchens.

So much choice. Yikes.

Not just benches and cabinets to be decided on, but sinks, door hinges, kicker boards, taps, storage.

For all his earlier enthusiasm, Milo quickly grows bored and starts trailing us, bowed over his phone.

I scan the showcase kitchens. "How do I choose?"

Jack leans against a stainless steel kitchen counter. "A budget will narrow your choices."

"Right. Makes sense. Well . . ." He patiently waits for me to give him a ballpark figure.

Milo has slunk off somewhere, and I savor the high cabinets that make it feel private.

"Mum and dad had paid off our house before they passed and they left a tidy sum of money for Milo and me."

"You don't have to tell me—"

"Just under two-hundred thousand. Thirty of it went toward the funeral. Milo has eighty-five grand in an account. Mine has a little less with these renovations. I bring in seven hundred a week from work, which pays for food and electricity, and the last year and a half I've squirreled three hundred away into a rainy-day fund. In that account, I have thirty-one grand."

The end of Jack's open flannel shirt is tucked under his arm and I tug the soft material free. "Impressive saving habit," he says.

"I don't pay rent."

"Nevertheless."

"I like security."

"Me too."

"How do your finances look?" Gentle heat prickles my cheeks, hopefully hidden by the scruff I didn't bother shaving today.

"Oh, Ben." He shakes his head. "What are we—"

"Was that an inappropriate question?"

His gaze pores into me. He rubs his beard. "I've been flipping houses for years. I've made a tidy sum of it. I have around a half million."

I laugh. "My figures seem pathetic compared to that."

"You're 24, I'm almost . . . I'm 39."

A sales assistant approaches us, halting the conversation. We decline help and move down the aisle. I want to say something about Jack seeming younger. Or maybe he could say I act older. Or, something.

"What kitchen styles do you like?" I say instead.

"Farmhouse. Vintage. Lots of exposed wood. Follow me, I'll show you." We arrive at a showroom with wide-plank hardwood floors, wooden cabinetry, and cream marble surfaces. The stunning L-shaped kitchen island has built-in seating. "This is pretty much my dream kitchen."

"The one for your villa?"

"It'll be worth the seventy-thousand-dollar price tag."

"Okay. We'll take this one."

Jack rubs his fingers on the marble island surface. "Ben, the cost—"

"I'll make it work, and you'll get practice putting in your dream kitchen. I'll think of you in your villa every time I microwave in there."

"Micro—Jesus. You cannot buy this beauty if you're only going to heat pre-packaged dinners."

"Then you'll use it when you visit."

"I won't let you blow your savings on this kitchen. Besides, aren't you going to sell?"

The question unsettles me, and I follow Jack around other kitchens unable to shake it off. Of course we're selling. That's the reason for the remodeling. Once the house is done, we'll move some place we'll be happy.

I stare at a ceramic tile counter.

"You okay?" Jack asks.

"Um, yeah." I can't look at him.

"You've gone quiet."

I force myself to flash a smile. "Can we think about the kitchens? You know, it's the heart of the home, so I want to make the right choice."

He frowns. He's reading me, but he doesn't probe. "Take all the time you need."

Chapter Thirty

BEN

IT'S WEDNESDAY AFTERNOON, A WEEK AND A HALF INTO THE new school term, and like the six days that preceded it, today is gloriously good weather.

Not a single cloud dots the sky. A sweet, spring breeze, smelling faintly of cut grass drifts lazily over our back garden. Birds chirp from the trees fringing our property.

The cottage roof, still unfixed, winks in the sunshine.

I bite my lip.

I turn on the deck chair to Milo who, splayed on the wood slats next to me, is writing notes about Aristotle.

We have two weeks left to perfect this assignment. No cutting and pasting this time.

My laptop hums on my lap as I switch from Aristotle facts to other very interesting Googly facts.

"Milo, come look at this a sec."

Milo heaves himself over and peers at my screen. "But that's Saturday."

"Yeah."

"We gotta—"

"Yeah."

Something bangs and shatters inside the house, and Jack curses.

"You good?" I yell out.

"Fine," comes his answer, followed by footsteps. Jack pops his head around the back door, and he eyes Milo and me. "Dinner will be half an hour longer than expected. Also"—he lifts his hand and jiggles his keys—"it'll now be takeout."

Milo fists the air in delight.

I might be doing the same.

Jack rolls his eyes. "I broke your casserole dish. I'll duck past the store and replace—"

"I have a better idea." I hook Milo's eye. "How about you hang out here, while Milo and I grab dinner and a new casserole dish?"

Milo's nose squishes. "I don't want to buy a new casserole dish."

I smile tightly at him. "Yes, you do. Casserole dishes are the best. They make Jack happy."

He slowly he starts nodding. "Oh. A *casserole* dish. Yeah, I want to buy a real good casserole dish."

Jack simply stares at Milo and me grinning at each other. "Just when I think I've figured you two out, you start a casserole mantra."

Chapter Thirty-One

JACK

I STRUGGLE TO SLEEP.

Ben seems to be struggling too. It's past midnight, and he's propped in bed with a laptop. Light beams onto his face, crunched in concentration. His hair is wild spikes, like he tried sleeping first but gave up.

He startles when he sees me upright on this bitch of a mattress.

"Am I keeping you up?" he asks sheepishly.

"You're fine," I say and, groaning, pull myself up. "I need a cup of tea."

Ben nods and swings his legs out of bed, scooping up his laptop. "Sounds good."

We pad into the kitchen and Ben sets his laptop down. In a week or three, all these cupboards and surfaces will be gone, replaced by another kitchen.

I won't let Ben spend his savings on my dream kitchen, yet it's the one I'm imagining as I sling teabags into mugs.

I rub my nape.

"Can you take a compliment?" Ben asks.

"I take complaints better." I switch on the kettle and turn around. Ben has his back to me, fiddling on his computer. His T-shirt is ruffled up his hip and his boxers cling to the tight globes of his ass. His shoulder blades flex as his right hand works the mousepad and keyboard.

"Here's some practice for you then: You are an extremely talented craftsman."

I pause. "But?"

Ben faces me. "*However*—" The dry look I throw him has Ben tripping on a chuckle. "However, I need to pay you more for your work. Free rent doesn't feel enough. Especially with everything you are doing for us."

I thought we talked about this. "I don't want to be paid to look after Milo."

"I just want to show you how much I appreciate you. I mean, the work you've done."

He's flushing, and I'm not immune to it. I've never been immune to it. "Do something? Like what?"

"Like redesign the blog you have on DIY projects."

I raise a brow. "Okay?"

His smile is a little too vibrant for this time of the night. "Cool, because I've already been messing around with some ideas."

He steps aside, and I spy the screen. A blast of color and designs from past projects I've made hits me. I move toward it. "That's . . . you did that?"

I scroll through what he's done and check out the menu.

"It's all your craftwork, just easier to navigate, and—"

"Amazing."

"Wait until you see the second idea."

He shows it to me, and all I can do is nod. I've always thought about getting more tech savvy with my blog but never got around to it. That Ben took the time to think of something that would mean something to me . . .

BEN LEANS IN, POINTING AT THE SCREEN.

"I put a birdhouse as a logo, but it could be anything."

"No . . . a birdhouse is perfect."

He's grinning at me, and I'm grinning back. The kettle whistles and I pull away to make us drinks.

"Now why can't you sleep, Jack?"

"Why can't you?"

Ben narrows his eyes. "Oh, you know. Still don't have a job that utilizes my degree and the second parent-teacher night, aka Judgment Day, is right around the corner. . . ."

"It's two weeks off."

"His assignment is due that day. I know Mrs. Devon will review it before I come in and if it's not perfect . . ."

"Ah." I hand him a peppermint tea.

"I wish you could talk to her for me."

"I wish I could do it with you."

"What?"

I burn my lip on a sip of tea. "Show me that second website again."

He shows me, but his gaze is hot on the side of my face, like he wants to say something else.

I peer out the corner of my eyes. "What is it?"

"I think I know why you're not sleeping," he says, carefully closing his laptop.

Our teas steam either side of the laptop and Ben and I face each other.

"I stumbled across some stuff while I Google-stalked you."

I laugh. "Right. Then you know."

One step, and Ben swallows the distance between us. He throws his warm arms around my neck. His chest is rising and falling rapidly against mine, and he swallows audibly.

My hands instinctively grip his hips. "Ben . . ."

"Can we?" he says hopefully. "As a birthday exception?"

It's impossible not to smile. It's impossible to press a single millimeter closer.

"I'd really like to wish you a happy birthday." His whisper pools at the seam of my mouth. "Many times over, if you're willing."

I chuckle, and he breathes it in, eyes darkening.

When I don't make a move, he shifts away.

I urgently clutch his waist, keeping him close. His eyes meet mine. The dried crack at the bow of his lip grazes my bottom one. "Jack?"

Words rumble from me, "Thank you for making this day special."

The scrape of his lips against mine makes me gasp. "The day's barely started."

"And still, it's the best one."

Door hinges groan and Milo's thumping footsteps push us apart. We're both half hard and Ben stares at me, horror washing over his face.

Milo is definitely approaching the kitchen.

I whip open the laptop and Ben jams his front against the counter. He types in his password and babbles. "No matter which version you choose, we'll have to reduce the size of the images to optimize page speed."

I have never wanted to laugh so hard. I mask a grin and glance at Milo wincing as he steps into the bright kitchen. "Thought I heard you," he says. His eyes adjust, and he steers them to me and Ben, and then the computer.

"Is it time to hand over the casserole dishes already?"

"Casserole—" It slams into me, and I laugh. "You know it's my fortieth too."

Milo smirks. "A little birdie told me."

Ben bubbles with a laugh. "Go grab our gifts for Jack."

Milo dashes out the room, and Ben yanks open the freezer and stands in the chill. "We're wearing pants to bed from now on. Thick ones. Maybe even those Mormon ones with the lock at the crotch."

I snort. "You got me gifts?"

"Milo put a lot of thought into his." Brotherly pride glitters in his eyes.

Milo returns a second after Ben shuts the freezer and nonchalantly slouches against the fridge door.

"This one's from me." Milo plants a wrapped box in my hands and gives the other wrapped gift to Ben.

I pick open the Sellotape as Milo bounces on the balls of his feet. "When are your birthdays?" I ask.

Milo explodes with impatience. "Who cares about ours when you're holding the best gift *ever*."

"We're both in February," Ben says. "A week apart."

Milo glares at him.

"What?" Ben says. "My gift sucks, I gotta give him something."

Grinning, I peel back the native-bird wrapping bit by bit. Milo shakes his head and I pull off the last bit in a rush and stare at an image of familiar binoculars.

"They're exactly like the ones dad gave us," Milo says. "Now you can join us bird watching."

These must have cost a fortune. I glance at Ben. As if reading my mind, he shakes his head. "All Milo."

"This is . . . Milo, thank you."

"Ben's briberies paid for them."

Ben smiles at his brother. "Can't think of a better way to have spent it, bucko."

"Can we all go to Zealandia tomorrow?" Milo asks.

Ben nods, then stops and looks at me, fidgeting with his gift. "Wait, do you have plans?"

"Luke invites me to dinner every year."

"Oh. Okay. Zealandia we can do in a few hours before that."

His disappointment is palpable.

Milo simply shrugs. "Get Luke to invite us to dinner too, Jack."

"Milo!" Ben growls.

"What?"

I cut over the space between Ben and me, and steal my gift. It's hard and pointy.

I haven't spoken to Luke about it yet. I wonder what he'll say. What he'll think.

It makes me nervous, but it's nothing compared to the belly-sinking feeling of leaving Ben and Milo here. "Of course I'm having Luke invite you. You didn't think I'd drag you two with me?"

"We're coming?"

"It's my birthday. I wouldn't have it any other way."

Ben steals his gift back.

"Hey," I say.

He shakes his head fervently. "I *so* gotta find you something better."

Chapter Thirty-Two

BEN

I HUM AS I SLING MYSELF OUT OF BED. HUM SOME MORE AS I call Talia.

I slink out to the back deck. Maybe Jack's working the garden again. I breathe in the energizing air of spring—

And freeze.

My phone rings distantly. I faintly hear Talia pick up.

Half my stomach comes up my throat as I speak. "Talia?"

"Yeah!" Her voice is upbeat and bursting with life.

I shut my eyes, but it doesn't make the clattering from the cottage any less distracting. "You're actually there?"

Talia laughs. "Very funny."

I want go back inside. Maybe even go back to bed and wake up all over again. This time to find Jack messing about in the kitchen or singing to Phil Collins from the bathroom. Or, I don't know, overhear him chastising me for leaving the toilet seat up. Anything. Not this.

"Ben?" Talia says.

I open my eyes and the same image greets me.

I inch to the edge of the deck. "When are you coming back?"

"You sound tired. You okay?"

"He's fixing the roof."

"Who's fixing the roof."

"*He* is fixing the roof."

"Oh. He. The One Who All Your Messages Are About."

"Not all."

"All."

I sigh. "The back cottage has a moat of old slats and nails. The morning sun is glaring off shiny new shingles."

"But a fixed roof is a good thing, no?"

My throat feels tight. "He's working so fast."

Talia sounds confused, "But you never wanted to stay in the main house. You can move back into the cottage sooner. Tonight, by the sounds of it."

Birds leap from the trees at Jack hammering. I can't say anything. Words have cemented to my belly.

"You don't want to move back," Talia says, realizing.

My mouth is dry. I stare up at the cottage roof, where Jack is crouched, his back to me. He's wearing canvas pants, boots, and a T-shirt, and he stops hammering and wipes his face with the crook of his arm.

Why is he working at lightning speed?

Why today?

It's his birthday. No one does chores on their birthday.

"Are you staring at him?" Talia asks, amused.

I snap my attention away from Jack to the budding lemon tree. It makes me think of the first night we met when he stayed by my side as I bribed Milo off the roof and how he's been by my side ever since. "Just thinking."

"Maybe you should stop thinking and start talking to him."

Gone for a year, and she still knows me so well. "What? I can't hear you. Bad reception."

"Liar."

I hold the phone a few inches from me. "Sorry, I can't hear you."

"Go chat with him, Benjamin," she calls out, laughing.

I plant the phone at my ear shortly. "Okay, okay. Later, Talia." I hang up.

I swing my gaze up to find Jack straddling the ridge of the roof, squinting over the yard at me.

A funny ache tugs at my gut. Just hours ago, Jack was sleeping soundly at the base of my bed. Now the distance between us feels vast and painful.

"Good morning," Jack calls.

I skulk to the cottage. "It's morning, I suppose."

"Careful, there are a lot of loose nails about."

I stop at his toolboxes. I want to look up at him but I can't.

"You all right, Ben?"

Jack steps down the ladder.

A panicky feeling has me whipping up something from the toolbox. I spin toward him holding it as a buffer between us. "What's this ruler for?"

He sets his hammer on the veranda and stops two feet away, amusement and sunlight streaking over his face. "That's a level."

Uh, dammit. "Just testing you."

"Of course."

He pinches the other end of it, and I swear it is a conduit of some kind, because I feel electricity pulse through it between us. "Well. Uh. Happy Birthday. Again."

Jack's brow gently pinches. "What's the matter?"

I steel myself against the thousand-plus volts. "I need you to level with me." We both look at the level, and I let my side go. "No pun intended. My brain is just . . . fried."

I want to smack my forehead.

"Level with you about what?"

My gaze smacks his and the question rips out of me, "Why are you fixing the roof?"

Jack sharply inhales and nods. He scans the garden and gestures toward the main house. "Maybe we should make breakfast?"

I want to throw up. "What a way to make me more nervous."

"No need to be nervous. Let's get some food and go from there. I haven't eaten yet and I'm starting to feel it."

I schlepp over the trimmed yard with him, trying desperately to keep the nerves out of my voice. "Shaky, feel it? Or, Godzilla stomping on Wellington city, feel it?"

He snorts. "Hangry, definitely."

I follow him inside. "Let's fill you up."

Jack whips up eggs and toast and steers me to the dining table. We've been chatting the whole time, but we both keep glancing at each other as we skirt around the real conversation.

A prickly quiet settles over us and every groan of our chairs feels ominous.

My heart thumps hard and makes eating impossible. All I think is that Jack is trying to find a way to tell us that he likes us. That he likes Milo and me a lot, but he thinks we need to pull back from each other. Redraw the line between us.

I should never have tried throwing myself at him last night. It was stupid.

"So. The roof," Jack begins.

He fixed the roof so we'd have more space between us again. I don't want to know. Really don't want to know.

"It's a sunny day," I blurt. "I get it."

"A sunny day, true, and—"

"You slept horribly. I heard you tossing and turning on

your mattress. You needed to put yourself to work. I get it. So, Zealandia. Are you ready?"

"Ben, we really need to talk about the roof."

I groan. "Yeah. But . . . it's your birthday. The roof can wait. There are more important things. Like cake and candles and making wishes."

"And opening gifts you hide in your nightstand?" Jack adds, brows lifting.

I prod at the eggs on my plate. "You don't want that one. It's . . . embarrassingly sentimental. I'll think of something better by the end of the day."

He laughs. "I suddenly know what I'll wish for."

I shake my head. "I've changed my mind about baking you a cake and putting candles on it."

"You were going to bake me a cake?"

"Don't look so worried. I can bake. What's your favorite kind?"

"Carrot."

"Resume looking worried."

Jack's smile is everywhere. His curved mouth, his pinched nose, his crinkled eyes. "I can make it with you if you like? We can take it as dessert to Luke's tonight."

It is one thing to serve cake to Jack, but it's another thing entirely to serve cake to Jack's friends, who are like his family. Who I *really* want to impress.

"Carrot cake. No sweat."

Jack grins. "Then back to the roof—"

"Milo!" I yell. "Stop playing on your phone, we're leaving soon."

Jack rubs his beard and leans back. He looks puzzled and possibly sad, but he nods. "Okay, we'll talk about it later."

I thank my stars this conversation will be put on hold.

I shovel eggs in my mouth.

"Can we leave in an hour?" Jack asks. "I'd really love to finish out back first."

Swallowing becomes a feat. Yet as soon as I've finished my mouthful, I take another. "Sure," I say, avoiding eye contact. "We won't leave until you're done."

~

THE WILDLIFE SANCTUARY IS BURSTING WITH LIFE. THE FLUTTER of wings, the murmur of wind, and the twittering of birds.

It is almost enough to take my mind off the roof thing, the carrot cake, and finding Jack a better present. Almost.

We stop by the café after a few hours' bird watching. Milo orders while Jack waits outside absorbed in a bulletin board. I pace the balcony overlooking the glittering reservoir searching for a free table.

"Ben?" The voice is male, but it's not Jack or Milo's. I spin and am greeted with an eyeful of guy in a gold bow tie and jeans, seated at the balcony banister. I recognize the dark hair and striking eyes immediately, but it takes me a sad few seconds to remember his name.

"Felix," he prompts. "From that embarrassing . . . evening." He winces. "Now I wonder what compelled me to stop you at all."

I laugh. "I remember now. The guy with four siblings."

"You remember?"

"It's a crazy number of kids, it sticks."

He's currently alone, but a second emptied cup suggests he's here with someone.

"We're leaving soon," he says. "If you want to snag our table."

Felix's gaze flickers to my right and a familiar warmth tickles my side. I take a large lungful of Jack's woodsy scent and start grinning like a fool.

Jack has his binoculars hanging at his chest and holds a folded piece of crisp white paper. He flicks the corner with his thumb as he eyes Felix closely. "There's a large, very vacant table inside."

I gesture toward the gothic water tower that stretches over the reservoir and the surrounding bush. "The view's great out here."

Jack darts a glance to Felix. "Not a bit cold? I wouldn't want Milo to get sick again."

Felix stands, bringing him closer to us. I suppress a violent, totally inappropriate urge to laugh.

"You're not putting us out," Felix said, dimpling. "We really are heading off."

"Great!" I say, and Felix starts pushing their cups to the side of the table.

Jack flicks the corner of the paper repeatedly.

"What's that you got there?" I ask.

Felix stumbles, and Jack pulls me out of the collision course. Jack's scent puffs between us as I'm crushed against him and the paper crinkles against my bicep.

Felix collects himself with a good-humored laugh, and Jack's fingers tighten.

I try to pick the paper from Jack, but he slides it to my elbow, drags it over my hip, and eases it into my back pocket.

His fingers seep heat against the curve of my ass, and my skin shatters into goosebumps as he whispers in my ear. "Read it later."

He pulls back from my ear, but his fingers lock on my ass as he narrows his gaze at Felix again.

Oh, fuck me. *Hell yeah.*

I know what's happening here. This is some awesome posturing, jealousy shit.

I want to whoop with delight.

Suddenly, the roof feels insignificant. Suddenly, every

moment, every look, every word between Jack and me triples in meaning.

Suddenly, I'm on top of the fucking world.

"Ben?" Milo calls.

Jack's fingers rip from my pocket.

I slam back to earth.

"Over here." I reluctantly wave him toward us. Milo gestures toward the café, speaking animatedly. "Mr. Campbell is here."

Felix makes a funny sound and I swing to his blushing face. "You know Mort, er, Mr. Campbell?"

Jack stiffly pivots toward the café interior.

I glance at the second empty cup and at Felix. "Small world. We've met. He teaches at Kresley Intermediate. How do you know him?"

Felix worries his bottom lip. "He's my . . . neighbor."

As if summoned, Mr. Campbell steps onto the balcony. He's all bright hair and smooth gait as he glides over to us, his gaze ping-ponging. He frowns slightly, and Jack tenses.

Three was already a crowd. Five is a mob.

I hook Jack's gaze. "You know, it is quite cold out here. We should head inside. I wouldn't want Milo getting sick again . . ."

THE MOMENT WE'RE HEADING BACK TO THE TRUCK—A TEN-minute walk—I start nudging out the paper in my pocket.

Jack ensures that Milo is out of earshot before stopping me with another dose of unveiled jealousy. "That guy back there . . .".

"Felix?"

"Is he a friend?"

Jack may as well have asked if I'd fucked him the way he chokes that out.

"He was a failed hookup."

Jack nods tightly and stretches his stride. I grab his arm and slow him. He casts me a sideways glance.

"Failed hookup. As they all were, Jack. Every single Friday."

His shoulders relax. He opens his mouth and shuts it again when Milo races between us, babbling about not being bird-christened yet.

"You're a kea," I say. "Clown of the mountains. Real annoying."

Milo pokes his tongue out at me, and I reciprocate like the adult I am.

Milo folds his arms, bunching his binoculars to his throat. "Seriously."

"You're a tui," Jack says, swinging his arm out to stop Milo stepping into oncoming traffic. When the coast is clear, we head down the hill.

"Tui?" Milo asks Jack, curiosity pinching his voice.

Jack confirms with a nod. "Three reasons for it."

My brows skyrocket along with the flutters in my veins. Jack's thought about this. I want to know why Milo's a tui as much as Milo does.

"Tell us, Jack," I urge.

Sunshine radiates strands of chestnut in his hair. A sparrow swoops over his head and settles on the picket fence.

Jack sweeps his grin from Milo to me and back to Milo. "Like you, the tui are boisterous."

Milo holds one finger up. "So far, so good."

"They're also noisy beasts for their size."

A laugh jumps out of me.

Milo narrows his eyes. "You have one last chance to decide if I accept your bird-christening."

Jack fondly messes Milo's hair.

"On the street, outside school," Jack says, glancing at me. "It was the first bird you tried to show me."

"The day you accused us of being Peeping Toms. Fond memory." I snicker, but I'm all uncontrolled warmth inside.

Jack smiles as if he reads right through me.

"Okay woodpecker, fantail," Milo says. "I'm a tui."

Jack and Milo chat about Jack's new binoculars, and while they're occupied, I pluck the paper from my back pocket.

"What?" I almost plow into Jack's back at the curb. "This is fucking perfect."

Jack scoots around the bonnet to the driver's side. "I thought so too."

"Like, beyond perfect. Like, my dream job."

Milo pinches the job advertisement from me. "You're going to work at Zealandia?"

I snatch it back with a grin, fold it into my back pocket, and slide over sun-heated upholstery after Milo. "I'm definitely applying."

Jack looks pleased. "Supermarket and home?"

I nod, then stop. "Wait. We're in Karori."

Milo shakes his head and speaks drily. "You only just figured that out?"

I pinch him. "No, I mean. There are lots of pretty houses in Kaori.'

Milo shuts up, and I waggle my brows at Jack, who starts the truck. "You want to see the villa?"

"As much as you want to show me."

IN SEVEN MINUTES, WE'RE CRUISING TO A STOP ON A SUNNY suburban street. I'm the first out of the truck. I stop outside the fence and take in the rose bushes and the heady scent of lavender that pokes through the gaps in the low, white-picket fence.

The villa gleams in the afternoon, a living version of Jack's sketches. Sketches I've seen so many times, it feels like I know this house. The paint has faded, the path up the garden is missing bricks, and the fretwork is broken in parts, but the bones are the same.

Jack lovingly smiles at his dream home and it makes me like it more.

Milo tugs my arm on my other side.

"Yeah?"

"We should hurry home." He avoids looking at the villa. "We have to bake Jack's cake."

I sense more than a need to bake, but it gets lost in the reminder that in three hours we are due at Luke's for dinner.

I wipe my clammy palms over the thighs of my jeans, feeling the outline of my phone. I have to make a good impression. I need to bake the best cake *ever*.

I'll need a foolproof recipe.

A foolproof list of conversation starters, too . . .

"Are you only going to admire it from the outside?" comes a croaky voice.

Jack and I twist to the elderly man sitting on the veranda, where a small kowhai tree had cloaked him from view.

"Howie!" Jack unlatches the gate. "You don't mind a few surprise guests?"

"Put on the kettle. I plucked some fresh lemon verbena this morning."

I'm all in. I scooch up the path.

Milo smiles shyly at Howie but otherwise keeps his head down as we enter the house and settle around the dining table for tea and cookies.

"How do you know each other?" Howie asks me, and I race a panicked look to Jack. What am I allowed to say?

Jack sits stiff in his chair, but he offers me an encouraging nod.

"We're, um, friends," I say. A slew of emotion crosses Jack's face, too fast to read. Did he not like me saying that? Or did he hate the lie as much as I hated saying it? "Jack is helping remodel our house."

Howie raises a cookie to his lips with a shaky hand, but his gaze is sharp. He watches us carefully over tea and hits Milo and me with a barrage of friendly questions.

Milo keeps his answers polite but short.

A flash of disappointment creases Jack's face. He schools it quickly, but I've already seen it. He wants Milo to love this place.

I want Milo to love this place.

While Jack converses with Howie, I nudge my brother. "The kiwi stained glass on the skylights are nice, don't you think?"

He looks up. "Hard to see through the dirt."

"A little clean up, and the gold of the kiwi will shine onto the dining table every morning." I gesture to the fireplace. "How cool to have an actual fire."

Milo shrugs. "Can you imagine all the spiders coming in with the wood?"

What I imagine is that $70,000 kitchen set, a long table stretching from the kitchen island, and Jack pulling a steaming roast from the oven. I imagine Milo and me sitting around the end of the table snapping a wishbone. Or working on school assignments. Or planning holidays.

I imagine the house at night, Milo sound asleep while Jack and I whisper in the dark. I imagine his body and mine colliding in bursts of sweaty passion. I imagine curling against his naked back and smiling between his shoulder blades until morning.

Heat rocks up my chest and I pluck my shirt.

Jack takes one good look at me and clearly reads my thoughts. His cheeks brighten, and his chair drags over wood as he stands.

"Milo, let me show you the best part of this house."

We follow him to a spacious garden fringed with native trees. Like a gift from the Gods, tui soar from the treetops to a small dried fountain.

I hang back near the house, while Jack and Milo tread toward it.

"I bet a birdhouse would look great here." Jack looks at me, and my breath comes out in short bursts.

We are thick in the middle of something. Thick in the middle of something special, and delicate, and frowned upon.

Howie clears his throat and I jump, because I hadn't noticed him slip to my side. A curious smile tips his lips, and it holds until we leave.

Milo and I trundle toward the gate, and Howie holds Jack back. I slow my step, keen to hear every word, and I do.

"This is not an official offer, Jack. But expect a call in two weeks."

Chapter Thirty-Three

JACK

THE CAKE COMES OUT OF THE OVEN TEN MINUTES BEFORE we're due at Luke's. Ben trundles it to the truck and races back, ripping his T-shirt off and mumbling about needing two minutes to change.

I double check I cleared all tools and trash from around the back cottage.

I stare at the back of the main house, momentarily transported to the villa. Milo had smiled once, hadn't he? At the birdhouse idea? Or had that been a trick of my imagination?

Two weeks. Two weeks, and Howie will give me a formal offer. As long as I don't fuck things up before then.

A light breeze steers me to the front of the house. Milo is struggling into his shoes on the veranda, and Ben is pacing by the truck.

The sun is setting, and warm amber light glows over the

street, bouncing off shingle roofs and seeping over the bark of newly budding trees.

Ben lifts his head skyward and murmurs, his corded throat flexing. He's changed into a fresh pair of jeans, a button-down shirt, and shiny boots.

He doesn't see me coming, lost in his thoughts, and I slow to admire him. "Okay, okay."

He pulls out his phone and twists his back toward me. It doesn't stop his voice from travelling the half dozen yards between us. "Google. What do I get my boyfriend for his birthday?"

I halt at the letterbox. My heart hammers. Not at the fact but hearing it aloud.

A smile yanks at my lips. I unlatch, step through the gate, and cheerfully snap it behind me. He jumps and stuffs his phone away. He's eyeing me, trying to determine how much I heard.

I cross to him and open the passenger door. We're standing face to face. "You ready?"

A gentle flush climbs his cheeks. He drags his fingers through his hair and nods. "Uh, Milo—"

"Can sit on your other side."

His gaze slips to my lips and my hands clutch the door. I burn to pull him in and kiss him. I have been burning for months.

Mrs. Devon's words pick at my brain, but they don't stop the feelings. Or the facts.

Facts Ben and I have to talk about. Tonight. As soon as we have a moment alone.

Ben's Adam's apple juts with a swallow and he climbs into the truck. I jump in the driver's seat as Ben hauls the cake from the dashboard onto his lap.

It smells delicious. "I can't wait to dig into that."

"We'll have to ice it first."

"You brought the ingredients?"

"Milo has them."

I hitch an arm on the bench seat behind him. Milo is straggling up the path with a bag.

I catch Ben looking at me. He shifts in his seat, and I tap my fingers against the upholstery behind his neck.

"What?" he dares.

My stomach riots, and I grin. "That gift you hid in your nightstand?"

His eyes narrow suspiciously. "What about it?"

I lean in and whisper, lips bumping on the curve of his ear. "That will do perfectly for your boyfriend."

He jerks back enough to search my face. I don't think I'll ever get used to the way his gaze plows into me. Like it reaches into my chest and fiddles around with my heart until it beats erratically.

I retract my arm as Milo trots to the door.

"Okay, party time," the kid says jumping onto the bench seat.

I acknowledge Milo and linger on Ben. "I'm ready to celebrate."

"Celebrate," Ben murmurs. "And ready to unwrap a few things."

OUTSIDE LUKE AND SAM'S, BEN STOPS ME FROM CLIMBING OUT. "Tell me things about your friends. I need to mentally prepare."

I ignore Milo's snicker and focus on Ben frowning at the darkened cabbage trees. "You'll be fine, Ben. Just be you."

"They won't like me."

"Of course they will. I'm very sure."

"You sound like you're trying to convince yourself. Shit. This cake better be magic."

If Milo weren't in the truck, I'd take Ben's hand and lock our fingers in a reassuring squeeze.

"What's the big deal?" Milo says.

Ben looks at me. I get it. This is as close as it comes to meeting the parents. Luke is my closest friend. Not to mention Luke was an ex. That's bound to make Ben more anxious.

Sure, they have met briefly, but brief waves in the classroom or on the soccer field aren't the same as spending an evening with them. Not just any evening, either. My birthday dinner.

I'm tempted to kiss away his fears, but public displays of affection absolutely cannot happen. Especially around Milo. As much as I trust Luke, he is also my colleague. Slips happen.

Simply inviting Ben and Milo here for my birthday dinner has raised enough questions.

Got to keep it friendly and platonic.

Got to avoid Luke's probing gaze.

Got to resist the insane urge to devour Ben.

I wring the steering wheel. "Shall we head in?"

"What about conversation starters?"

"Dude, you're being weird," Milo says. Cool air washes over us as he cracks open the door. "Just come inside. If you get stuck, gloat about your awesome brother. Or chat soccer stuff. Ohh, say how you think I dribble the ball like a pro. Because I do, right Jack?"

I roll my eyes and leap out of the truck. Milo and I cushion Ben at the front door. Luke opens and welcomes us into the entrance.

Ben's grip seems to double on the cake carrier when Luke smiles at him.

"I brought the carrot," Ben blurts, and gestures toward Milo. "And he dribbles. A lot. It's impressive."

Luke looks at him confused. "That's okay, we have napkins."

With every ounce of composure left in me, I fight to keep my face impassive. "Milo, take the carrot cake and follow Luke."

They slink down the hall, Milo mumbling.

When they are out of earshot, Ben groans. "I brought the carrot? I think I insulted myself."

I check we are alone, and fold Ben into my arms. Not one minute inside, and I'm bending my own rules.

He sighs against my neck. "I want to go home. I can't look at Luke again. You'll just have to get new friends."

A laugh rumbles out of me. "We'll make it short, promise."

I pull back, and Ben sneaks in close again. "We'll talk later?"

"I wished we'd talked this morning."

His chest expands. "The roof."

I hold my fingers an inch apart. "I'm this close to playing hooky so we can talk now."

"What's stopping you?"

"Cake."

Ben nods as if this makes sense. "You're a man after my own heart."

I grin. "I meant blowing out the candles on the cake and making a birthday wish."

"You really want that sad gift I made?"

Made? "Christ, yeah."

Ben strides down the hall toward the chatter in the great room. "I got this."

Chapter Thirty-Four

BEN

I DON'T HAVE THIS AT ALL.

The moment I step into the bright room, I stall. Not because Milo has casually flung himself on a sofa, smelly feet planted on a delicate gold cushion—although that's not helping to better our impression—but because Sam and Luke are softly kissing in the kitchen.

Their sweet, open affection makes me long for the same.

Jack steps beside me and I stare at his hand cupped to his hip, thumb in his pocket.

"Crazy in love those two," Jack says.

The comment has Sam pulling out of Luke's arms. He wishes Jack happy birthday and greets me warmly.

I'm hyper aware of how dry the roof of my mouth is. I hope I don't cluck before speaking, and that when I do speak, I sound like an adult.

"Going to offer me a beverage?" Jack asks. "Or do I help myself?"

Sam laughs. "What's your poison?"

"Water will do. Driving."

I lean toward him. "It's your birthday. Have a beer or three, I'll drive us home."

He studies my face. "You don't mind?"

"Go for it."

Luke opens Jack a bottle of beer, I score a Fanta, and we all drink.

Luke tries to snag Jack's gaze, which Jack suavely avoids.

The two are otherwise at ease in each other's company. Of course they are. They used to date. They've shared histories. They know what each other looks like naked. *They've had sex.*

How is Sam so relaxed, sipping his whiskey, listening to them banter?

Jack and Luke have done the horizontal tango!

Imagining them together is stupid and inappropriate. I don't even know what Jack looks like naked.

Does he imagine sinking into me as much as I imagine sinking into him?

Jack frowns and snaps a hand to my forehead. "You okay? You're looking flushed."

I burn harder. What do I do?

Laughter.

It's the best medicine.

I rut out a laugh. "I'm good. Just warm in here." What is the current conversation, anyway?

I spy the exit.

Luke eyes Jack and me again, and his expression flickers. Wait? Does he think we're together? Suspect it? Why does he try so hard to tell Jack things with his eyes?

Is he imagining *us* naked?

I wonder what we would be like naked . . .

"Ben," Sam says, "what is it you do, exactly?"

What is it I do?

My eyes widen as I search my brain for an answer I shouldn't have to search for.

"I do Te Papa!" I clear my throat. "I work at Te Papa—it's a wonderful museum, but I'm scouting around for something more personally fulfilling."

Holy shit. It's like I've never met people before. This level of nervousness will kill me.

Jack looks like he wants to laugh and curl me close. God I wish he would. I spin my can of Fanta and almost topple it.

Thankfully Jack catches and steadies it.

Sam tells Milo to help himself to the snacks on the table.

Frustration rockets through me when Milo hums and doesn't look up from his phone. Seriously? Am I that bad a caregiver he has no manners?

Jack doesn't look all too impressed at Milo either, and I feel doubly shit. When Sam returns to the kitchen, I slink to the sofa and nudge Milo.

"What?"

I channel my inner Jack and pinch the phone out of his hands.

"Hey!"

I berate him under my breath. "Look at our hosts when they address you, bucko." I slide his phone into my pocket. "Feet off the cushion. Come with me and make small talk."

"The likes you are making?"

I swat the back of his head and we move to the kitchen island. I ask Sam if we can whip up icing for the cake. It's the perfect escape from making a fool of myself, and I'm happy when Sam hands over the necessary utensils.

Milo pokes my side and steals the bowl. "I can do the icing, Ben," he says loud enough for the others to hear. "You go back to chatting."

I smile stiffly. "You sure, bucko?"

"One thousand percent."

I mutter at his ear, "You're doing this on purpose."

Milo murmurs back, "Maybe you'll think twice about teasing me about Kora."

I knew that would come back to bite me in the ass.

I growl, but it's more playful than I'm pretending. At least he can give as good as he gets.

I return to Jack's side.

"What do you think about the new elective for next year?" Luke asks him.

"The philosophy round table?" Jack laughs. "I think I'd love to mediate."

Philosophy?

Sam says something I miss, and suddenly everyone is staring at me. Okay, so we're talking philosophy. Not my forte.

Oh, wait. "Philosophy! Yeah. Like, did you know Aristotle thought the heart was the center of intelligent thinking? I mean, not technically correct, but I think he has a point!"

Over Sam's shoulder, Milo has stopped mixing ingredients and is staring at me. Yep, I'm stealing this word for word from Milo's assignment. I'm the worst role model in the world. "He also thought the direction of the wind could change a goats' sex!"

Milo looks horrified. He throws me a lifeline and turns the electric whisk on high, drowning any other stupid words that might tumble from my mouth.

Fuck.

A warm hand sneaks to the back of my thigh, covered from sight by the island. Jack is looking toward the food Sam is preparing, barely suppressing a grin. He squeezes me gently.

Sam and Luke laugh politely and muse about other weird philosophy facts.

This evening is disastrous.

Through dinner, I bow down to the powers of Smile and Nod. I'm the first to start clearing the table and working on the dishes, despite Luke's insistence it's fine to leave them.

Jack picks up a dishtowel. "You two cooked, we'll clean." He faces me. "You've gone quiet."

"I'm sorry for messing up this evening."

He turns on the tap, water rushing into the sink, hitting metal. "Are any of them looking at us?"

I scout over his shoulder. All three of them have migrated to the sofas and only the backs of their heads are visible.

I shake my head.

Jack hums. "Good." He's a foot away, and suddenly he's right there. His lips graze mine, soft and tender like a breeze. Like a whispered declaration.

My lips part on a sharp breath, and his tongue touches mine for a fraction of a second before he pulls away. Our eyes hook. Jack reads my surprise and the desire bubbling through me, and I read his warring emotions. He shouldn't be doing this here. We could get caught.

He glances at my lips again, and I see the curse silently seep out of him.

He taps a finger against his mouth in the sign of 'be quiet', and then he's everywhere. His mouth collides with mine, his hand clutches my waist, his other hand massages my nape. I grip his biceps and pull him tighter. His leg slips between mine and we silently deepen our kiss, tongues sliding together, urgently, fervently. His fingers slide up the base of my hair, and I drag mine to his elbow and squeeze.

He feels incredible. I want more. I want our bodies sliding together, his weight on me, mine on his. I want tangled limbs. I want to feel every inch of him, breathe him in, taste him.

I want to gasp.

I want him to shudder out a moan.

It's a kiss of seconds, but they are the best kissing seconds of my life.

We pull back.

"You didn't mess anything up."

I flush and glance at our hosts and Milo. They are unaware of our stolen moment, lost in their own conversations.

Jack and I do the dishes, chasing each other with looks and silent laughter.

"You guys make dishes look fun," Sam says, coming into the kitchen. "What's your secret?"

Across the room, Luke snorts and Jack throws him a look.

"Cake," I declare. It's the only word I've got.

As promised, no sooner the candles are blown out, Jack does his sickie thing.

Fifteen minutes later, Milo, Jack and me are bundled up in the front of the truck.

Adrenaline sloughs out of me and I wipe the sweat from my brow. It's done. I survived.

"Oh." Almost forgot. I flash Jack an exhausted smile. "By the way, your friends are cool."

Jack laughs.

Chapter Thirty-Five

JACK

AT HOME, BEN AND I SEND MILO OFF TO BED, AND HEAD outside for privacy. For the talk I wanted this morning. The talk I played hookie to have now.

We move across the darkened garden to a ladder that I left angled against the guest cottage. Ben sticks close to my back and releases a breathy laugh that trickles through my hair. "We're going up?"

"It's flat and sturdy. We can sit up there to talk."

I test the ladder's positioned safely before climbing. At the moonlight-soaked roof, I brace the top and call Ben up.

"Roof's definitely fixed," he says as he reaches the top.

I steer him safely onto the shingles next to me. He mirrors my sitting position, legs outstretched toward the gutter. Shingles press coolly against my palms and seep through to the backs of my canvas pants.

Ben's side bumps mine. We're both in shirts but jackets

might have been sensible. We'll have to settle on scooching closer. When my leg rests against his, Ben smiles. His breath mists in the air, and he stares through it at the burgeoning backyard garden, and the back of his bungalow.

I follow his gaze and admire the corner property. The house is crying for new paint, the kitchen is yet to be fitted, and more garden work is necessary, but it feels warm and welcoming.

Ben's voice is deep and shaky, "We're boyfriends."

He stares at the house, and I stare at him.

"How did that happen?" He faces me.

I'm hit by the tender awe in his gaze. I feel it too. "Bit by bit since the first day we met, Ben."

He nods, and his voice lumps with emotion. "When did you realize we were more than friends?"

I slide a hand on his thigh and rub over the inner seam of his jeans. "On some level, since the albatross."

Ben groans and presses his forehead against my shoulder. I wrap an arm around his shoulder and tap my thumb on his bicep.

He peeks up at me. "When did you know for sure?"

"The moment water poured into the cottage and you moved into the bungalow with me. Although I tried to deny it."

"When did you stop denying it?"

His hair combs my lips and I drop a kiss on the top of his head. "Our first date."

He pulls off my shoulder and stares at me. "We had a first date?"

"At the café. Precisely the moment we ordered a second coffee. You asked me to make memories for Milo with you."

Ben smiles. "God, you teased him mercilessly."

"I'd do it all over again."

We watch the neighbors return from their night out. Breezes ruffle our shirts and an owl hoots in the distance.

Ben strokes my index finger. "Why didn't you say anything earlier?"

I sigh, turn up my hand, and weave our fingers together. "I'm still figuring things out."

"The complicated situation with work?"

"School policy discourages this. I'm in a position of authority. I have to think how this looks to my colleagues and other parents."

"How it looks?"

"There's sixteen years between us, Ben. You and Milo are living a difficult phase in your lives. Is it fair to start a relationship with you right now? Is it fair to emotionally involve Milo if this ends in three months?"

His voice pinches. "This'll end in three months?"

He tries to remove his hand and I grip his fingers. "*You* may want to move on. That could hurt Milo. And . . ."

"And?"

"What if the last memory I have of you boys is your sorrowful look as you wrap an arm around Milo and shut the front door in my face?" My voice breaks. This is the invisible rope that has been holding me back the most. "What if I lose my family all over again? Yes, family." I lift our entwined fingers toward the main house. "Because that's exactly what we're playing here."

Ben swallows. "Is that why you fixed the roof? Because you want to stop playing?"

I laugh drily. "No, Ben. I don't want to keep using it as an excuse." My breath heaves out of me. "I fixed the roof because although it's complicated, although I could lose my job and my dream house and the respect of my peers, I need to know."

"Know what?"

My voice stammers. "May I play family with you for real?"

The following silence tugs tenderly. I've never been so afraid of a response. I look at Ben and I see a future. I see shared dinners and overshared stories. I see stupid fights and silly gestures to make up for them. I see him and Milo in the villa. A family to laugh with during the day. A partner to moan with during the night.

The dream hangs between us.

Ben palms my jaw, fingers touching my exposed cheek above my beard. He steers my face until I'm looking into his warm, dark eyes.

"I've had to grow up fast the last two years. I know I fuck things up and do stupid things, but I know what I want, Jack. I want kind. Good. Solid." He presses a single, tight kiss to my lips. "I want you."

I close my eyes and feel my lungs expand on fresh air.

Ben continues, "I know you have a lot to lose. What if we keep things G-rated until Milo has finished at Kresley?"

"I'm not sure I want to wait that long," I admit. "But yes, until I've figured out exactly how to broach this to the school faculty, we should try harder to act—"

"Like we're just friends. Maybe you should move into the guest cottage."

I don't want to.

"I overheard Howie, too. He's planning to offer you the house in two weeks."

A strange mix of hopefulness and anxiety mashes in my gut. "A small slip from Milo at school would set the dominos rolling. I was reckless earlier."

Ben accepts this with a blunt nod. "Then it's settled. No more touching until you've signed the dotted line and purchased your dream home."

I will figure out how to deal with this at school. First, the villa, though.

A lemon flies at us and I catch it before it smacks into Ben's face.

Ben and I jerk our attention to Milo, who is in his pajamas

and bare feet hopping on the cold ground next to the lemon tree. "You're supposed to be in bed," I say.

Milo pretends not to hear me and focuses on his brother. Like he thinks he'll have more luck with him. Kids. "Where's my phone?"

I'm tempted to tell Milo not to play either of us to his best advantage, but I know Ben has this. He has this just perfect.

Ben's posture straightens, and he confidently calls down, "How will your phone help you sleep?"

"Please? It's Saturday. The *weekend*."

Ben plucks the unripe lemon from my palm and tosses it as his brother. "Get to bed, bucko."

Milo duck-jumps out of the lemon's path, giggling. "That'll cost you twenty bucks."

"You're out of your mind."

"Ten?"

"Get in your bed or no media for a week."

Milo blinks at Ben. "You're kidding."

"Does it look like I'm kidding?"

Milo whirls a panicked face on me. "Mr. Woodpecker," he whines. "You broke my money machine."

I smile proudly at Ben, and yell down to Milo. "Better listen to what he says, mate. Your brother isn't joking."

Milo scampers inside, and I laugh.

Ben catches my eye. "The day you tell the school about us?'

"Yeah?"

"I'm telling everyone we're together. And I'm fucking your brains out. Probably not in that order." Ben crawls toward the ladder and swings his legs onto it.

I follow, bending to hold the top as he climbs down a few rungs.

He pauses. "Jack?"

"Hmm?" Our faces are inches apart. His tongue darts over his bottom lip.

Soon. Soon.

"You still have a pathetic gift to claim."

"I need a walk first. I'll come in when I'm done?"

I take twenty minutes staring at the night sky, then trek through the town belt, burning off the energy dancing in my veins.

Control gathered, I quietly slip into the house. Milo's snores are semi-muted by his closed door. The shower drums in the distance, then shuts off as I head into the bedroom.

The curtains aren't pulled together all the way and moonlight slithers across the bed. Shadows from the trees sway on the wall and ceiling. I sit and turn on the bedside lamp.

My gift sits atop the nightstand. I want to rip into them, but I won't give in to this or any other impulse.

Ben shuffles into the room gripping a towel around his waist. Waterdrops fall to his shoulders and roll into his matted chest hair. He eyes me and the gift, and I see his groan in his slumping shoulders. He pulls out a pair of boxers and glances at me over his shoulder.

He doesn't know if he should drop the towel in front of me, but he wants to. He's my boyfriend. It's frustrating to have to worry about the physical aspects of our relationship.

"Hurry up, then," I say, throwing him a grin. "I want to open this."

The towel slaps wetly to the floor and I'm treated to an eyeful of his profile. His smooth, muscular ass cheek, dark red curls surrounding a half-hard cock.

I lurch off the bed and snatch up a bag.

"What are you doing?" Ben asks, confused. The elastic of his underwear snaps.

With quick yanks, I unzip the bag on the end of the bed. "I figure I should pack some essentials for moving into the guest cottage."

"What about your gift?"

Ben holds the wrapped gift toward me with a knowing glance to my crotch.

I school my expression of lust, and try to pluck the gift from him. He jerks his hand back, closing his fingers around the base of it. "Just . . . lower your expectations, okay?"

"Gimmie."

He hands it over and jumps into bed covering the blankets over his face.

"That reaction makes me more curious, Ben."

He peeks out. "You're torturing me on purpose. Rip it open and have done with it."

I sit next to his covered feet and open. I laugh, and Ben kicks my hip through the sheets.

He glares at me, and I temper my grin. "You whittled this for me?"

"With my pocket knife and a chunk of wood I found in the conservatory."

"Ahh, from the wood I had purposed for a replacement doorknob."

Ben pales.

"Just teasing. Thank you for this . . ."

He shuts his eyes. "You're holding it up the wrong way."

I turn it around and spot what is possibly a beak. Or a sword. "Is this a woodpecker?"

"Well it's supposed to be." He forces himself to sit, the blankets ruffling to his lap. "God, I feel so dumb giving that to you. It feels silly and childish, like something you give to a crush."

I rub his foot through the blanket. "All the more special. It's made with a skipping heart, shivery skin, and silly smiles."

He laughs softly. "All butterflies and shyness, all right."

I set it on the nightstand. "Thank you."

He grabs my shirt as I pull back. I still. He looks over to my opened bag, grip crumpling my shirt. "Stay with me tonight?"

"Ben . . ."

"One last night before you move into the guest cottage? Just sleeping."

I hesitate. I'm in control, I can sleep alongside and Ben without anything happening.

"The door is shut. For all Milo knows, you slept on the mattress, and nothing has changed between us."

"He's in the next room."

"We're only sleeping."

I give in.

Ben is watching me, but I concentrate on peeling out of my clothes. I keep my underwear on and shimmy into a sleeping T-shirt.

Ben switches off the bedside lamp and I crawl into bed next to him.

His heat leaks toward me, and I shuffle to maintain a good foot between us.

Ben rolls onto his side and I lie on my back, staring at the shifting shadows.

"Goodnight, Jack," Ben says.

"Night, Ben."

I keep my eyes shut for a few minutes. Ben's breathing becomes slow and regular. I shift quietly on my side and peek at Ben's sleeping form.

Only, he isn't sleeping. He has an arm under his pillow supporting his head, and he's admiring me, the softest smile on his daydreaming lips.

He slowly trails his gaze over my lips back to my eyes. He stills when he finds me watching him back, but he doesn't look away. His dark eyes hold mine. One beat. Two beats.

I'm moving. He's moving. We collide together.

Lips bump, hands pull and pluck and roam, legs tangle.

I roll on top of him.

He's flushing and beautiful and sexy.

He clutches my biceps like I might suddenly slide off him.

I'm not in control. I don't want to be.

He glances toward the wall that separates us from Milo's room, and his voice is a plea as he whispers. "We'll keep quiet."

His eyes beg me to continue.

I kiss the fuck out of him.

Chapter Thirty-Six

BEN

I PINCH THE HEM OF HIS T-SHIRT AND JACK SHIFTS FOR ME TO draw it over his head. I drop it on the bed and shimmy Jack's boxers over his stiff, plum-headed dick. I quickly remove his underwear and he helps shirk mine off too.

We clash into a kiss. Jack lowers me down, and my back folds to the cool sheets.

I suck in a sharp breath as Jack's thick cock slides against my own. I push up into Jack's warm, broad weight.

Jack combs my hair off my face and cups my head. His palm nestles atop my ear.

I recognize the slew of contradictory emotion passing over his expression. Hungry lust hoods his eyes as if he doesn't thrust against me he'll go insane. And he's looking at me tenderly, lovingly. Like I'm the most amazing man he's met and simply looking at me will suffice.

I feel the same.

My lips part on a breath, and he dips his head. His lips skim mine, and I suck in his exhaling breath. His other hand clasps my hip as he grinds against me. Intense arousal makes my cock throb, and I slide my hands over the smooth plains of his back and urge him tighter against me.

The hand at my ear disappears as Jack repositions, sinking his chest to mine. One of his hard nipples meets mine and the hairs on our chest graze together, eliciting a shock of goosebumps.

Jack buries his head into the crook of my neck and nibbles my throat. His beard scrapes over my skin along with the wet dart of his tongue. I buck as my nerve endings light up. My cock pushes against the base of his navel, leaky with pre-come. My hands roam his flexing muscles, and I pull him closer.

I pant, trying to keep quiet, and his breath is ragged in my ear too. Our hearts thump together, excited, nervous.

Jack drags open-mouthed kisses over my jaw to my chin. He nips it and meets my eye. I cup the back of his neck and clamp his ass cheek as I steady myself through the whirling, intoxicating desire pulsing between us.

I can't look away from him, and I don't want to.

He reaches a hand between us and pushes open my thigh. His leg rolls warmly between mine. Our erections slide together, and our balls tap. I hitch my leg around his ass and press him to grind more, harder.

Jack's breath stutters against my nose. He holds back. "Ben?"

"I want you."

He surges into a frenzied thrusting and I grip him through the throbbing ride. Our toes push, our calves bump, our nipples comb, and our cocks rub. Shivers ripple over me, growing more powerful.

I lift my face and snatch a kiss. Our tongues dance slickly

and Jack slows his thrusts to a gentle grind. It is everything I have missed these last months in one achingly passionate kiss.

I drop back to the pillow and thrust a hand between our bellies. The head of his cock bumps the pad of my thumb and leaves it moist. I curl a hand around us and relish in Jack's shudders as I stroke.

"Christ . . ."

The praise in his utterance rushes through me. I push Jack up, steer his legs either side of mine, and wriggle under him. His arms flex as he braces himself against the mattress, and I drag my lips over his tangled chest hair and his tight stomach to my prize. I kick the blankets off the bed and palm the tight globes of his ass. He smells salty and sexy, and his straining cock twitches against his abs as I release my breath.

Fuck, I want to ravish and be ravished. I want everything we've been denying ourselves. Everything we might have to restart denying ourselves tomorrow for the unforeseeable future.

His cockhead bumps against my lips and then slides over my tongue. He hisses, and it's loud, and I know we have to keep it down, but I want him to lose control again. And again and again.

I grip the base of his cock and I suck him deep. He's so fucking hard, and he's shaking with the need to cant his hips and fuck my face.

I want him to, and I sneak a finger down his crease and rub over his entrance. He shallowly lurches into my mouth, pulls out, and does it again. On each withdrawal, my finger probes harder against his hole.

I love his eagerness. His responsiveness.

The million and three things I want to do with him . . .

My throat works as Jack pushes deeper and deeper. It's so arousing, I abandon Jack's ass and greedily grab my dick pumping in time with Jack.

He pulls out of my mouth, and his firm calloused hands manhandle me expertly up the bed again. His kiss sears through me and he swallows my moan.

I whisper against the lip I've sucked so hard it's swollen. "Please, Jack?"

His gaze drills into me. He lowers his mouth to my ear. "Drive or driven?"

Both. Either. But . . . the way Jack moved when I touched his ass. I push against his chest. "Drive."

He rolls to the bed and I twist for the nightstand. I find the condoms I bought for the sex-ed talk with Milo, and Jack's lube. Jack's on his front, shoving a pillow under his belly. The curve of his ass beckons and I'm so hard, yet I'm also trembling with nerves. I want to sink into Jack, but I want it to be great for him, too.

His face is on the side and he's watching me, reading me.

He whispers deeply, "Slick us both up and lie on top of me."

I slip between his parted thighs and stroke lube over my cock. I breach him with my lube-coated fingers and instantly he writhes under my touch. I pour plenty of lube between us and cloak myself over Jack's hot back.

"Your hands." Again, a whisper. Everything between us is a secret.

Our arms press together and like the first night we shared this bed, he catches my fingers and curls them tight with his. My palms suction onto the back of his hands. He moves our hands either side of his shoulders, bracing me comfortably behind him.

My cock slides between his lubed ass cheeks and I rut my shaft against his entrance as I drop kisses between his shoulders.

He shifts his face and lightly bites the knuckles on my left hand. It chases sensation through me and my groan seeps around the curve of his neck.

I free my fingers from him and steer him onto his knees. I scroll my thumbs down either side of his spine and part his ass cheeks.

I nudge my cock against Jack's tight ring, feeling it give as he relaxes, ready for this to happen. I'm quivering for it to happen too, and I drape myself over him as I inch inside his slick, tight hole. His shiver vibrates through me and I stop and whisper if he's okay.

He parts his knees and quietly moans for me to move.

His channel grips me as I sink all the way in, and I whimper.

I pull out and slowly bury myself in him again.

I'm living one of the fantasies I've had of Jack and me. Only this time when I slide in and out of him, there's a thousand times more sensation. The cool air of the room waking over our bodies, the give of the mattress under my knees, the sensual way the moonlight drifts through the curtains over Jack's flexing back, the pulsating pleasure in my cock on every instroke. Our soft puffing. The restraint of that one sense, magnifying all the others.

I wrap a hand around Jack's cock and tug him slowly, making him shudder and jerk with suppressed grunts.

I pull him up against my chest, and his dense weight claps against my chest. I kiss his throat at the base of his ear. Jack reaches behind us, plants firm hands on my ass and drives me into him. A gasp wrenches out of me, and Jack turns his face and kisses the sound from me.

My chest seizes with uncontrolled breaths and urgency throttles through me. I piston into Jack harder, faster. We fall to the bed and I'm pinning him to the mattress as our pleasure furiously crescendos.

Jack grunts heavily as he comes over my fingers, the pillow

muffling his sounds. But there is nothing to mute mine. I snap into him, skin slapping, as I chase after my orgasm. He clenches his ass around me and I slam into the most intense pleasure of my life. A shout leaps out of me as I spill, rooted deep inside him. "Jack," I moan again.

He finds my hand and holds my fingers to his lips as I lie draped over him, catching my breath and clarity of mind.

Worry trembles through me. I shouldn't have yelled Jack's name. "Sorry," I whisper.

Jack twists around and I slip out of him. He's sticky and the condom squishes between us, but I don't care. He tucks me against his side. Shyness sneaks up on me and I stare at his chest, unable to look at him.

He gently steers my face to his. "That was damn hot, Ben. I wanted to shout too."

"Do you think he heard?" God, the thought is awkward.

Another good reason for the dining room to become the new master bedroom. More space between rooms.

Not that it matters for Jack and me, because Jack is moving to his villa, and we will sell soon, too.

I frown and bite my raw lip.

"We'll cross every bridge as they come," Jack says after an audible swallow.

He shifts against me as he pulls the condom off my soft-ened cock. He quietly slides out of bed, trashes it, and steals into the hall to the bathroom. Floorboards creak as he returns, and I hold my breath, hoping the sound doesn't carry. Hoping Jack isn't more aware of each noise now that desire is out of the equation. Hoping he doesn't decide to sleep the rest of the night on the mattress, or worse, hike to the guest cottage.

Jack reaches for our boxers, tosses me mine, and slips into his.

I wrangle mine on, and Jack rolls back into bed beside me. He mirrors me lying on his side and pulls my leg over his thigh.

His fingers trial lightly over my hip to the base of my spine. "Do you really have a list of all the Phil Collins songs I sing?"

I flush, hard. "Only on my phone."

He swoops in, laughing, and kisses me.

I'm flooded with the need to whoop. To yell. To blast how happy I am to the world.

I compress it to a grin.

Chapter Thirty-Seven

BEN

THE NEXT MORNING OVER WEET-BIX AND COFFEE, I STARE AT my brother, trying to read his every expression. Gauge his reactions. Had he overheard anything? Does he suspect?

"Why are you looking at me strange?" Milo says, not looking up from his bowl.

"What? I'm not. Nothing strange happening at all!"

He glances at Jack who has leaped up and started piling our dishes. Jack has been extra careful not to share any lingering looks with me. It's almost enough to make me question if I dreamed last night.

The next weeks—or however long we have to keep this secret—will be agonizing. I'm kinda hating it already.

But I'm determined to respect Jack's tricky situation. "So, Jack," I say. "The guest cottage roof is fixed."

Milo stiffens on his seat. "We're not moving back in there are we?"

I'd assumed Jack would take our place in the guest cottage. Because . . . because there's more room in the main house for Milo and me, and he's happy in his old bedroom.

Jack balances our plates on one arm. "Of course you aren't, Milo. I'll move there, and you can have your space here."

"Does this mean an end to eating your dinners?" Milo asks. "Because you cook so much better than the microwave."

"What a ringing endorsement."

I snicker as I eagerly wait for Jack's answer. How do we navigate the appearance of a platonic friendship?

Jack plucks up Milo's bowl and adds it to his pile. "I still have a fridge full of groceries. I can't be assed moving them, so consider me your cook for the next week."

"Can we sneak Fanta back into the fridge?" Milo asks.

I begin to nod but Jack's tight stare stops me. "Nope. Not so much as a can." Jack twists for the kitchen and I lean in to Milo. "Are you kidding? We are totally stocking up."

"I heard that," Jack says from the hall.

Milo and I smirk.

THE FOLLOWING TWO WEEKS GO BY AT A SNAIL'S PACE. IT'S strange having the bedroom to myself. I miss Jack's light snores sending me off to sleep. He's here for every dinner and hangs around most evenings to watch TV with us or play board games. But he retires before Milo goes to bed and there's never a moment to drop the friend façade between us.

The one time I tried sneaking to the cottage, Milo caught me at the backdoor after awaking from a nightmare. His scar gleamed in the light, and guilt sucked me right back into the house.

I hug my towel headed for the bathroom as Milo exits his

bedroom yawning. "You're showering again? Didn't you do that last night?"

"I'll explain when you're older."

I leave him with his innocent frown to jump in the shower and work my aching wrist.

I dress for work and startle when I see the time. Fuck, I was in the shower longer than I thought.

"Milo!" I yell, popping my jeans' button into place. "We're running late!"

I scurry into the hall to find Milo slipping on his jacket, his school bag ready at his feet. Jack is waiting, flipping his keys.

"*You're* late, you mean," Milo says. "Jack saw your car outside and came in to check we're okay."

"Fuck, Jack, now you'll be late too."

Jack looks like he wants to offer Milo a ride so I can go directly to work. He holds back, and I stifle the small thread of disappointment. "We'll all make it."

I grab my wallet and keys, slip into shoes, and race with Milo to the hatchback. Jack drives his truck toward school and we follow behind him.

My brother rests his head against the passenger window, and his reflection shows him smiling. It's a glimpse of a Milo that has been happier these last months. A glimpse of a kid who is cheeky, and silly, who talks back, who unofficially marries his brother outside an outhouse, who has pre-teen crushes on girls.

I reach out and gently punch his arm. He looks over and I grin.

"What?"

"Did you stuff Aristotle in your bag?"

He hauls said bag onto his lap. "Why else would it be bursting at the seams?"

"Along with all his other infamous qualities, he's a contortionist as well. Make sure to mention that to Mrs. Devon for extra points."

"I do that, and you'll hear about it at parent-teacher night tonight."

"Yes, maybe she'll finally admit how charming you are."

He squishes his nose, but a glimmer of hope shines through. He shrugs. "I wouldn't count on it."

"Well what does she know? Other than math and science and geography?"

"How to freeze your insides with a single look?"

"And that."

Milo grins. "Thanks for helping me on the assignment. I love how you tested it out on Jack's friends."

I slow behind Jack at a stop sign, wincing. He studies us through his rearview mirror and it does fluttery things to my gut. "Could we, like, forget the embarrassing shit?"

It's green, and I release the clutch too fast. We stall.

Milo hoots. "Like this?"

Fuck.

Of course Jack notices and pulls over on the other side of the intersection.

I curse and restart, scowling at Milo's unabashed giggling.

But secretly, I feel relieved.

He trusts that I have it under control. He's at ease with me in a car.

I cruise past Jack acknowledging him by blinking my lights. He slides in behind me, and it's my turn to peek at him in the rearview.

"When will you tell him you love him?" Milo asks, and I slam on the brakes. Jack halts behind me, throwing me a confused look. I rein in my surprise, wave a meek apology to Jack, and continue winding down the hill, flushing furiously.

"What do you mean?" I ask Milo, tightly.

"Come on."

He's figured it out. Fuck, he has to keep it secret. "It's . . . that obvious?"

"Uh, do I have to remind you of the voicemail fiasco?"

I recall. "Okay, um. Sure, Jack's attractive and I'm crushing on him. But that's it. We're just friends."

"Pull my other leg."

My hands are clammy on the wheel.

Milo continues, "I mean, it makes sense. Jack's made for you."

I swallow, and apparently that says everything.

Milo smiles like this makes his day, week, year. "You should tell him."

"Well . . ."

He reads me. "What? You've told him? Why the hell is he in the guest cottage?"

"It's complicated."

"He doesn't love us back?"

I park in front of Kresley Intermediate, since this time we're running late. Milo stares expectantly at me, worry filling his eye.

"Jack makes us dinner every night. He comes bird watching with us, he takes you to the soccer field to practice your dribbling and to give me a break, he confiscates your phone at the dinner table."

Milo bites his bottom lip.

"To me that sounds like a man who very much loves us."

A hitched sob-like giggle pours out of Milo. "Seventy-three. That's the number of sentences he started with 'Ben's the best because . . .'"

He laughs, and I store that info behind a smile.

"So why is he living in the guest cottage?"

"The timing isn't right."

Milo looks toward the school. "Oh. *Oh.* Because of me."

"You have to keep this quiet. No one can know. Especially no one from school."

Milo frowns. "For how long?"

I slump back against my seat and sigh. "I don't know."

He looks at me long and hard, his expression tight. He nods suddenly and opens the door. "I'll take the bus home and meet you after parent-teacher evening."

He climbs out and looks back in at me. "Hiding your feelings is not okay, Ben. We've done enough of that."

I'm too surprised to reply, and it's only once he's halfway to the school entrance that my stomach lurches.

Chapter Thirty-Eight

JACK

IT'S BEEN HARD HAVING MILO IN MY CLASSES THESE PAST couple of weeks. Every time I look at him I'm hit with the breathless feeling that he's family. That I get the privilege to help Ben raise him into adulthood. That he's mine, too.

It's hard keeping my voice firm when it needs to be. Harder not to beam with pride. Like in today's woodwork class, where he's instructing Devansh on the differences between rasps and files, and when to use each.

Milo drops the file that he's holding when Kora struts past him toward the wrenches, and I stifle a grin and the blatant adoration on his face.

"It's my religious belief that she's made for me," he says on a sigh. I clear my throat and his gaze sharpens on me. "What?"

I stop roaming the class and tap the workbench at his side. "We really need to discuss the meaning of religion."

Milo shakes his head and mutters, "We really need to discuss the meaning of *love*."

I calmly continue around the classroom, but my stomach has balled into a hard knot. Every minute to the bell drags painfully. When it rings, the kids scamper toward the exit. Milo tries to duck out, too, but a curl of my finger has him slinking back inside with a bowed head.

Maybe I should wait until after school, but I'm unusually anxious. "Is there something you wish to say to me, Milo?"

He crosses his arms and perches on a high stool.

"What's up?"

He whispers, "For someone who claims to love us, you're really stupid."

I suck in a shaky breath and crouch to maintain eye contact. I guess the cat's out of the bag.

"What do you mean?" What Milo thinks means everything to me, and the accusation in his dark frown pummels my gut.

"It's been so long he's faked it. Now he has it for real, how can you make Ben hide it?"

"Hide what?"

"Being happy!" He blinks rapidly and his jaw twitches like he's holding back from yelling at me. Like he's hurting.

Worry yanks through me. "Is this about keeping our relationship quiet?"

He rolls his eyes. "Duh."

I grip the lip of the table beside us. "It's not that simple, Milo. Many teachers and parents won't like our situation. And that beautiful house we visited in Karori? I've waited years for it. If I acknowledge things too early, I could lose that. I promise, it won't be long now. I'll figure it out. Okay?"

He blinks. "So your villa means more to you than we do?"

"No."

"Oh, you want *both*. Us and everything."

"Milo—"

He continues, his frustration morphing to anger, "You don't want to take the high road, don't want to be bereft of anything."

"Wait—"

"I have four words for you, Mr. Woodpecker."

I brace myself for them, but they plough guilt through me. "*Shortcuts never end well.*"

I'M NOT IN THE MOOD FOR HANGING OUT WITH STAFF OVER lunch. I'm headed for my truck to call Ben, when Luke catches me in the middle of the netball courts.

A rain shower has ceased, but a chill wind remains. Our boots squelch through puddles.

"What's up, Luke?"

He side eyes me. "That's my question."

We're alone on the empty courts. Nevertheless. "We can't have this conversation."

"You can't keep avoiding the elephant in the room forever."

He knows. Of course he knows. We dated for years, he knows my tells. "Not forever, just a bit longer."

Luke braces a comforting hand on my shoulder and steers me to look at him.

His warm, friendly gaze churns my insides.

"Jack, please."

A salty gust howls over us. My boots snick as I walk toward the back gate. Luke keeps quietly beside me.

I stare toward the tree where I spotted Ben bowed over the innards of his car. Then toward the street stripes where he chased his empty bottle. Then toward his usual parking spot, where he has a great view of the netball courts.

Luke isn't giving up, and I don't want him to.

At my truck, I lean against the wet trailer. Luke slouches against it, too, an elbow cocked onto the railing.

I spy him and refocus on the school. "Do you think it's wrong, how much time I've been spending with Ben and Milo?"

He snorts. "You're the happiest I've seen you in years."

"What if it's more than friendship between me and Ben?"

He barely blinks. "The teacher-caregiver thing doesn't bother me a bit."

"But?"

"No buts. Not exactly."

"Spit it out, Luke."

Luke wavers over which words to pick.

I sigh. "Is it the age difference? Mrs. Devon has already warned me about taking advantage."

Luke lurches away from the truck. "The fuck? That woman needs to mind her own business. You're the most decent guy I ever met, after Sam. Ben is an adult. You're an adult. On that level, what you do is your own business."

Relief swamps me. "So why'd you hesitate?"

"Getting involved with a guy who has a kid . . ." He smiles tenderly. "I did that. It comes with its own set of obstacles."

I close my eyes and see the pain etched into Milo's face.

I've never felt so horrible. It glues my gut, and it's why I need to call Ben.

Luke continues, "Kids have a whole host of emotions and a totally different filtering system. Sometimes they don't understand adult decisions and they can get mad and"—Luke's expression shutters and I know he's speaking from experience —"it can rip you up inside. I just, I want to help. I want to support you. But, damn you, Jack, you've got to let me."

I shove my hands in my jacket pockets and take that in. My back bores into the ribbed siding of the trailer. "It's been a while since you cursed at me."

He snorts. "Well overdue."

"Yeah."

Luke sweeps me into a back-clapping hug. "Ask me anything. I'm on your side."

He pulls back and I nod.

"I'm fairly sure I'm already fucking up the caregiving part."

Luke smiles fondly. "Welcome to the club."

"I thought you were supposed to be helpful?"

He laughs and slinks backwards toward the gate. "Parenting fuck-ups are as inevitable as the sun rising in the east. But with every sunrise comes a fresh start."

"How very Master Yoda of you."

His eye sparks. "Let's watch *Star Wars* together some time."

"You, me, and Sam?"

"Or me, Sam, Jeremy, you, Ben and Milo."

My pulse trips over itself. "It's a date."

"One I hope happens sooner than later."

He twists and hikes off.

I dive into the truck and call Ben. He answers on the third ring, huffing. "Jack? Fuck, this is about Milo isn't it? He figured it out, I didn't tell him. I mean, I confirmed it when he asked, but only because he totally knew."

It saddens me he's so worked up about this. That I'm the reason for this anxiety. I rest back against the bench and shut my eyes. "I'm not calling to accuse you of anything."

"I was going to leave you a message during my lunch break."

"Are you on the clock? Should I call later?"

Air skips down the line with his breath as if he's on the move. "It's okay. I'm ducking out five minutes early. Twenty seconds to privacy. Tell me something."

"Luke figured it out as well. He took it well."

"Okay, outside. So your friend knows. Milo knows. How many others, do you think?"

He sounds hopeful about the prospect. There's a spark in his voice and all I can hear is Milo's anger about how I'm forcing him to stifle this happiness.

"Look, Milo said something at the end of class today."

I give him a quick overview of the conversation. "I'm concerned about what I'm asking of you—"

He clears his throat. "Milo sees the world more simply. I know there are stakes to revealing our relationship."

I ground the back of my head against the headrest and use his words. "The adult stuff sucks."

"Tell me about it."

"Ben—"

"I'll see you at school later? Or not. Dinner, then. Unless you have plans with staff."

I frown. "Dinner, definitely."

We say goodbye, but it doesn't feel very good at all.

THE SUN COMES OUT AND SUCKS UP THE PUDDLES, BUT EVERY hour that passes has me more and more uneasy. School ends, and parent-teacher evening begins. Seeing each parent grin over their child's work crushes me with envy.

I want that.

I could *have* that.

I check the time. Ben should be arriving for his meeting with Mrs. Devon soon.

I straighten already straight toolboxes. I wash my hands and hesitate as I pick up the towel. It's the replacement one Ben bought me. I massage it against my head.

After a few steadying breaths, I calmly lock up and head to the staffroom.

My phone vibrates and thinking it's Ben, I pull it out. It's Howie.

It's so tempting to answer him, and I do.

"Finally," he says. "The call you've been waiting for."

I want to hear it so badly. It takes colossal resistance to speak. "Wait, Howie. You need to take a moment before you offer it to me."

His voice is gravelly and curious. "Why's that?"

"I'm about to chat with your niece."

"I fail to see how—"

"She won't like what I have to say, and I'm afraid that might influence your decision."

He is quiet for a beat. "When are you talking to her?"

I clear my tightening throat. "I'm a fist away from knocking on her door."

"Take me in with you."

I reach out to knock and Principal Ryan opens her office door. She startles. "Jack. Are you finished with parent-teacher evening?"

"I need to talk to you."

"Can it wait, I—"

"No."

She steps back and gestures me inside. I step in and she shuts the door behind us. She glances at my phone, and I press speakerphone mode and rest it on her desk. "It's Howie."

"Is this about the villa? Has he officially offered it to you?"

Not yet, and who knows if he will. "He'd would like to listen in."

She settles behind her desk, frowning. "What's going on?"

I pace before her, perspiring. Her office is all desk and shelves. Blinds are drawn against the evening sun. It's warm in here. Stifling.

"Jack?" she prompts.

"You know I'm working on a renovation project for Milo McCormick's home."

Her pose stiffens. It takes a beat before she speaks, and

when she does her voice is all principal. "I've said it before, you are a valuable member to the community."

"This time is not like other times I've helped parents."

She looks at me warily.

I grab hold of the frayed chair opposite her desk. "I didn't keep it professional. I couldn't. The more I was around Milo and Ben, the more involved I become in their family. And the more I got to know Ben, the more our relationship evolved."

"Are you saying you're dating Benjamin McCormick?"

"I'm saying I'm in love with Benjamin McCormick."

I'm breathing heavily, waiting for her or Howie to reply.

She does first. "This will be a sensitive issue for some people. Ben, being a past student of ours and the age difference between you . . . It will slant some teachers' opinions."

"And yours?"

Her jaw locks. "He was a student when I first started at Kresley, Jack. He sat in that very chair you're strangling. He made a strong, immature impression. One hard to let go of."

"He's an adult now—and a mighty fine one at that."

"There is nothing to prohibit you from dating a caregiver."

Horrible sadness thumps through my veins. She wishes there was.

"This isn't just dating, Stephanie," I say quietly.

"We can only hope that makes things easier to accept." She stands, clearly telling me it's time to leave. It's a punch, but I expected it.

"I am a good teacher. I care about the kids. I'm committed to this school and always have been. I also want a life outside Kresley, and I found it with Ben."

She takes this in with a sigh, and nods.

"I saw you with them boys, Jack." Howie's voice bursts from the phone and I pluck it from the desk with trepidation.

"Howie, I'm sorry if this conversation makes you uncomfortable. I don't want to come between you and your niece."

"Jack? I think I ought to chat to Stephanie and call you back."

"Yes," I rasp. "Of course."

With one last look at Stephanie's tight face, I gather my wits and take my leave.

Chapter Thirty-Nine

BEN

WHY AM I SO WORRIED?

I stride over the sunset-glistening quad toward the soccer field, my stomach flip-flopping like a washing machine. I'm on time for my meeting with Mrs. Devon, I'm wearing an appropriate shirt, and I know exactly where Wing C is.

I thought the nerves were supposed to cease if I have my shit together?

A breeze dances behind me, urging me toward the classroom. I take a cursory glance toward the industrial arts building. The lights are out. Looks like Jack has wrapped up his parent-teacher hours. His truck was still parked out back, though.

I shake off the quickly spiraling thoughts of Jack. Of the last time I had parent interviews. That first moment we met . . .

Got to keep focused.

I schlepp my way to Mrs. Devon.

All the lights are on and it takes a moment to adjust to the unflattering brightness. The room is neat, as always.

Mrs. Devon adjusts her large glasses and checks her watch.

"I'm not late," I say.

"I know," she murmurs. "It must be a first."

"Probably." I grin weakly. "It won't be a last."

Student assignments are piled nearby. Milo's Aristotle project sits on top. There's a scrawled note stuck to it and I rip my gaze away. My palms are sweating. It can't be another two points out of eighteen, surely? We ticked off all the requirements.

I know it can't be as bad.

I still want to throw up.

"Milo McCormick. It's been a big year for your brother."

"A couple big years."

A flash of sympathy crosses her face. "It was a rough beginning for him here at Kresley. He used inappropriate language in class, disturbed other kids from their work, did the bare minimum."

"A flashback from my time here, huh?"

"Quite. However, the last couple of months he's shown startling improvements. He's paying attention in class—even participating in discussions. He's showing better social maturity. His friendship with Devansh should be encouraged."

Pride rips a flush up my neck.

She continues, "Perhaps our last conversation set things on a better course? Something at home must have contributed to these positive changes. Whatever that is, keep it up."

Mrs. Devon picks up Milo's assignment. "I took a glance over his newest assignment. I've not settled on a grade yet, but I am very impressed. I think—"

"I'm a good caregiver, Mrs. Devon."

"Excuse me?"

I take a breath and look her in the eye. "I'm not perfect. I've struggled. But I try my best. I am a good caregiver."

"I'm not sure what—"

"Sorry I keep interrupting you. I really need to get this off my chest. The last times we've been together, I came away believing the worst in myself and my abilities to look after Milo."

"I'm sorry if I have been blunt, Mr. McCormick."

"You were. Now I need to be blunt." I rub my palms over my jeans. "Something at home has certainly contributed to Milo's positive development. We have support." The classroom door snicks open. A parent checking if we're done or not, probably. I don't stop to look. "We have someone in our lives who believes in us, who helps me be a better parent, who helps Milo grow."

"Someone in your lives," Mrs. Devon repeats, frowning.

I hate that frown. "Yes," I say. "Someone wonderful who we love."

She's still staring over my shoulder.

I follow her gaze and my body jolts.

Jack is in the classroom.

His gaze hooks on mine, bursting with tenderness. He glances at the chair beside me, a question in his eye.

I nod.

He sits and his Adam's apple juts as he reaches for my hand. "I'm sorry I'm late." He defiantly faces Mrs. Devon. "How can Ben and I best support Milo's learning?"

Mrs. Devon glances uneasily between us.

I choke Jack's hand. "You're here? You're actually here?"

He rubs his thumb over mine. "Right where I'm meant to be."

∼

I'M FLOATING ON LOVE. I'M FLOATING SO FUCKING HIGH, I'M out of oxygen and speechless.

Somehow, I drive home, tailing Jack's truck the whole way.

Somehow, I get into the house without mauling him.

I shakily call Milo's name, and he answers from his bedroom. Good. He's there. Jack's here. We're all here.

Jack's phone rings as he's removing his boots. I sneak my fingers into his pockets. His back is warm against my front and I soak it in as I pull out his phone. He clasps the phone and my fingers against his chest. "Take this call with me?"

"Who is it?" I ask.

"Howie. About the villa."

I practically skip him to the kitchen. "Answer, answer."

Howie's voice slices between us. "Jack."

"Howie."

"Can I be blunt and to the point?"

Jack grunts out a laugh. "You always are."

"Aye. You finally found a partner. Have a family."

Hearing it from a third source is surreal and awesome, and I snap my legs around Jack's hips and urge him closer. He smirks and shifts close, holding the phone between us. He's warm between my thighs and I can't wait for later, when there'll be no clothes between us. Just his skin slapping against mine as I beg him to fuck me senseless.

"Yes," Jack says, and I'm sure he's answering my thoughts as much as he's answering Howie.

"Gosh, it's been a long time since I've seen such blatant, beautiful love," Howie says.

"Wait," I pipe up. "You knew, too?"

"Ah, Ben, hello."

"You really knew?"

"I've lived a long time. I know love when I see it."

"Are you calling to officially offer Jack his dream home?" I blurt.

"I always wanted Jack to be happy," Howie says. "Jack. The villa is yours if you want it."

I grin wildly at Jack. He hasn't lost his villa *and* he's made our relationship official. I can't fly much higher than this.

Jack is beaming. I can see him picturing his perfect house with us in it.

"Are you imagining all of us living—" I start.

"Yes."

Howie starts talking about the discussion he had with Principal Ryan and how she'll eventually come around. Jack scoots to the opposite bench and hunches into that part of the call and I sneak out of the kitchen.

I need to tell Milo the good news. Jack and I aren't hiding anymore. Jack got offered his villa.

I've got to excite Milo about the possibility we might move in with him.

Wood bounces underfoot as I rush into his bedroom. He's not there. I hear Jack's faint voice as he wraps up his call with Howie in the kitchen, and something else. A shuffle.

A gurgling sound has my senses on alert, and a nervous tug in my gut says I know where I'll find Milo.

I pause at Mum and Dad's parted door.

Milo sits in the same spot between windows where I sat months ago. He's cross-legged, head bowed. Evening light soaks stripes of bronze into the room, but Milo is wedged in the shadows. He's still in his school uniform, all gold and navy and bright purple socks.

He catches me sighing and swipes his eyes. He shrugs. "I overheard the news. Woodpecker and fantail have been set free."

I laugh gently and slouch into the room.

His eyes glitter wetly. "Jack gets his villa."

I sit next to him and wrap an arm behind his shaking shoulders. "What's wrong?"

Milo swallows and drops his forehead against my arm. "I'm trying to be happy for you."

"You're really looking the part, bucko."

He chuckles and shakes his head, wiping his runny nose on my sleeve. "I am happy for you. I am. But all I can think is . . ."

I gently pull away to see him. My voice comes out thick and apprehensive. "What did you think?"

He rubs the heels of his hands against his eyes. "I hoped you'd come around. I hoped you would decide you love this place. I hoped we'd be a family here."

I swallow a sigh. Exactly what I feared Milo would say.

His bottom lip wobbles, and sympathy pummels me every time he presses his lips to control it. "But Jack loves his villa."

"Milo—"

"And you love Jack."

"I do—"

"And I love you both. So"—he shrugs—"I came in here to get the guts to be okay with it."

My throat pinches. "Oh, you Gryffindor. Come here." I haul him out of the shadows and into a crushing bronze hug. "I love you, Milo."

He hiccups against my shoulder, and I stroke the back of his knotted hair.

I see Jack hovering outside the door. Our gazes lock and I know he overheard it all.

It's hard to breathe. Jack's been waiting on his villa for over eight years. He loves every inch of its timbered frame.

But, if he wants us to move in . . .

I shake my head at him. I can't stop shaking.

Jack's chest puffs with a heavy breath, and still, I'm shaking my head. "I'm sorry."

Milo pulls out of my hold frowning, and I refocus on him. "You're *happy* here. You need this place." I silently beg Jack to understand. "I'll always choose what's best for my bucko."

Milo's voice is hopeful and uncertain. "What are you saying? We're staying here?"

I don't know where this leaves the future Jack and me, and the fear is paralyzing. But I do know that Milo and I aren't leaving. My throat is too tight to speak, and I nod.

Milo throws his arms around me again, sniffing and giggling.

Jack smiles softly and quietly retreats. I hold Milo as tight as I can.

SAPPED OF EMOTIONAL ENERGY, I STEER MILO TO HIS FEET.

He beelines into the kitchen, and I freeze in the doorway. Jack is crushing garlic into a pan of sautéing onion. The homely scent of dinner unfurls hope in my belly. But seeing Jack juggle pots and pans isn't enough.

Jack smiles at my brother, and then spots me. He holds up a finger over the hiss of the pan, fiddles with the element knobs, and moves toward me. He's taken off his flannel shirt. His canvas pants sit low on his hips and his T-shirt is tight enough to show off his muscles.

I can't look up from his chest. What if needing to stay here and not eventually moving into the villa is a deal breaker? What if this is our last supper?

Jack stops before me and I can't bear what he's about to say.

At least, not until . . . "Milo, get me a Fanta?"

The fridge snaps open and shut, and Jack confiscates the can just as Milo's passing it to me around his side.

"Are you insane?" I say, trying to swipe it off him. "Can you not see how vulnerable I am? If I don't get that can, my world will end."

Milo and Jack do a duo snort that has me yanking my head

up and scowling at them.

Jack teasingly waves the can.

"You play a dangerous game, Jack."

His laugh vibrates through me, heavy and seductive. The hope in me escalates.

Jack cracks the lid and takes a tiny sip. His face contorts, and he hands it over. "That stuff'll rot you."

I curl myself around the can protectively. "Shhh, you're talking about the love of my life, here."

"Fanta?"

I take a sip. "Who'd ever have thought love could be so fizzy?"

His gaze washes over me. "Or so orange."

I charge into the kitchen, dump the can on the bench, and whirl back to Jack.

He lifts an amused brow. "Thought you needed to drink or your world will end?"

"It will."

My hand fists his T-shirt. I haul him close. And then I'm kissing him.

I'm kissing him over and over, drinking him all in. It's not enough to quench my thirst and I wonder if it ever will be.

Out the corner of my eye, Milo moves. He's snickering, and I don't give a damn. Neither does Jack. His arms wrap around me and he is kissing me like he wants it to last forever.

Eventually, I unhook our lips. "But what about—"

He kisses me again.

I laugh and pull out of it. "—your dream home?"

"Yes, well . . ." He eyes the ancient stove, the narrow counters, and the aged fridge. "It needs a better kitchen." He taps my nose and the love in his eyes pours into me. "Otherwise it's perfect."

"You mean . . ."

"I called Howie back and declined his offer."

"You what? But it's your dream. You've waited forever."

He pulls me in and whispers in my ear. "I'm *always* going to choose what's best for my two boys."

This time I don't contain it to a grin.

I fucking whoop my lungs out.

Epilogue

JACK

BEN WILL BE STRIDING IN FROM THE LAUNDRY ROOM ANY MOMENT.

Cardamom, cumin, and a hint of cinnamon waft from our open-plan kitchen. The casserole in the oven will be ready in an hour. Just in time to have my wicked way with Ben.

"Oh my God, Jack, what are you wearing?"

I jerk my head toward the kitchen door. Milo has a big, shit-eating grin on his lightly-bearded face.

Christ. I thought he was spending the night with his girl-friend. I glance down at Ben's old dragon-boating uniform that I found while Marie-Kondoing our drawers. "Your brother asked me to wear it."

"And you blindly followed orders? Emphasis on blindly. You'd have to be to squeeze that on—and keep it on."

He sneaks to the fridge and grabs a Fanta. Still not kicked the habit, but at least the sugary indulgences happen weekly rather than daily. He cracks open a can, looking at me. His eyes are all laughter.

"You weren't meant to see this."

"Any way I could un-see this?"

"Okay, smart ass, that's enough. For every comment out your mouth, I'm telling Jasmine stories. Like the time you first rolled home drunk, while Ben, Talia and I were planning your birthday and you—"

"You know what, the whole look is growing on me."

I laugh. "Get outta here."

"What?" Milo fakes outrage. "I graduate *yesterday* and you're already kicking me out of the house?"

"For an entire night, too. God knows your brother and I deserve it."

He laughs. "I'm grabbing a change of clothes and heading to Jasmine's. Tell Ben we're still on for bird-watching tomorrow morning. Six am."

"Jasmine will love you."

He exaggerates a sigh. "I can't believe I'm dating a night owl. But I suppose no one's perfect."

He shakes his head at my outfit again, and his smile shifts from amused to something weightier.

I get the feeling he knows something that I don't.

"What?" I ask.

"Just . . . you're the best, Woodpecker. Have an amazing night." He disappears, whistling.

I shake my head and grin after him. What an incredible young man Milo has turned out to be. Solid, dependable, confident, witty. He'll go far in life.

He's already planning a year abroad to Europe and Canada.

My smile wanes and an ache pulls in my chest.

He grew up too damn fast.

Ben reappears from the laundry room, shuddering. "Forget

'if it makes you happy!' Three of everything. Three pairs of socks. Three changes of pants. Three T-shirts—"

He erupts into a laugh. "When I said 'I'd love to see that on you,' I was joking."

"I'm surprised I got the shorts up past my knees."

Ben stops in front of me and picks at the hem of the shirt clinging to my navel. "This uniform brings back fond memories."

"You were so worried Milo would knock up his first crush."

"The knocking-up worry hasn't gone away!"

I share the fear, but it never lingers. I trust Milo to be safe, and I know Ben does too.

I cup Ben's prickly face.

He sighs against my lips. "I can't believe he's finished school. I can't believe he's eighteen."

"Me neither."

"I can't believe I'm thirty."

"Forty-six," I groan. "I always win this game."

Ben drags his lips over mine. "You don't look a day over forty."

I growl and nip at his laughing lips.

The front door snaps closed. Milo's off. The house is ours.

Good.

I haul Ben against me, steering his thighs around my hips. He hardens against my stiffening cock. I deepen our kiss and bathe in Ben's heavy, pleading moan.

I pull back. "I gotta get out of these clothes."

"Do we need scissors?" Ben helps me strip and I take my time torturously helping him.

He's panting by the time I free him of his boxers.

He's begging by the time I've finger-fucked lube up his ass.

I crowd him against the eggshell wall. He gasps as his back meets it and greedily bites my lip when I steer his arms above his head.

He locks his legs around me and arches perfectly. I thrust my aching cock into him, croaking in pleasure. He's slick and tight and made for me.

Curses bounce out of Ben on every thrust.

Our eyes meet, dancing with desire, need, and love. I sink into him and pause to kiss him. I will never get enough of this man in my life.

The one I laugh with during the day.

The one I moan with at night.

He's beautiful and he's mine.

BEN

JACK POUNDS INTO ME UNTIL I'M A LOUD, BEGGING MESS.

He cants his hips harder, faster, sawing against my prostate. My back rubs against the warm wall and his hands dig into my ass cheeks. I clench around his thick cock, orgasm building, and Jack throws his head back, corded neck flexing.

Jack grips my leaking dick and pumps, his thumb flicking over the head—

"Jack," I whimper, as my balls draw up.

He snaps his hips three more times, chasing his orgasm. Release plunges through me, and Jack chokes on a groan and spills inside me at the same time I coat his stomach in come.

He sinks against me, smacking my stomach with stickiness.

I slide my hands over his sweat-damp biceps and kiss him between pants. "Just for the record, we're fucking hot together."

Jack laughs and chases me with kisses as we clean up in the bathroom and slip into clean clothes. He doesn't stop kissing me until the casserole begs his attention.

"Will you celebrate seven years working at Zealandia with your workmates next week? Should we throw a dinner party?"

"You think?"

"Talia asked as much. She wants an excuse to party."

I love how Jack and Talia get along so well. Love how Luke and Sam have become as important to me as they are to Jack. We have a freaking awesome family.

I jump onto the marble counter and taste dinner off a wooden spoon.

"What do you think?" he asks.

I lick the sauce again. He's watching me with wry amusement.

"I think . . ."

He raises a brow.

"I think we should do it all over again."

"What? Let me try it."

I hold the wooden spoon hostage. "Not the casserole, Jack. I want to have kids with you. I want us to do the parenting thing all over again."

My breathing grows ragged as I wait for him to say something. Anything.

He's not even smiling.

Jack palms the marble either side of me. He stares deep into my eyes. I've never once seen Jack cry in all the years we've known each other, but a tear now damps his lashes. "You once asked me to remind you never to have kids of your own. You said it's all silent treatment and uncomfortable conversations."

"And an insane amount of worry—I know what I said, and I was right. But I want to do it again anyway. With you."

The kiss comes suddenly and desperately, and Jack is pulling me close. His voice is broken. "We'll foster?"

"Probably better than plucking one off the street."

"You've really thought about this?" His hope is palpable.

"We can also try for adoption. In which case, I have picked out names. Robin for a girl. Jay for a boy."

"Bird names?"

"Have you met me?"

His laugh settles. "What will Milo think?"

I draw back with a guilty grin. "Um . . . I kinda asked him what he'd think if I suggested this to you."

"That explains the funny smile he gave me."

"He was here?"

"He's still up for birdwatching tomorrow."

I smile. "You coming with us?"

Jack's eyes are glittering. He swallows. "Yes."

"Great, I might have to borrow your binoculars, mine are bust—"

"I'll come bird watching, too. I mean, *yes*, Ben." He smiles into a kiss that will chase me with shivers forever. "I want to do it all over again with you."

~ THE END ~

Acknowledgments

I couldn't have written this book without the rock-solid support of my hubby. You are an amazing dad, and I love navigating this parental adventure with you. We're both Bens and Jacks, and we love our Milos. ;-)

As always, you are my inspiration for writing romance. You set a high bar, love.

Vir, Sunne, Teresa Crawford. Thank you for all your tremendous guidance to help shape this story. All my hugs!

Cheers to HJS Editing for all the fantastic edits and the fast turn-around. And thank you to Wolfgang Eulenberg for proofreading, and Vicki for being a wonderful final eyes reader.

Lastly, big thank you to Natasha for designing the cover. The boys' love really shines through.

Anyta Sunday

HEART-STOPPING SLOW BURN

I'm a big, BIG fan of slow-burn romances. I love to read and write stories with characters who slowly fall in love.

Some of my favorite tropes to read and write are: Enemies to Lovers, Friends to Lovers, Clueless Guys, Bisexual, Pansexual, Demisexual, Oblivious MCs, Everyone (Else) Can See It, Slow Burn, Love Has No Boundaries.

I write a variety of stories, Contemporary MM Romances with a good dollop of angst, Contemporary lighthearted MM Romances, and even a splash of fantasy. My books have been translated into German, Italian, French, Spanish, and Thai.

Updates on my projects can be found at anytasunday.com.